*Meet Me*

**M**

Copyright © [Year of First Publication] by [Author or Pen Name]

All rights reserved.

No portion of this book may be reproduced in any form without written permission from the publisher or author, except as permitted by U.S. copyright law.

# Dedication

I dedicate this book to my son William who makes us laugh every day.

# Contents

♥

| | |
|---|---|
| Prologue | VII |
| 1. Chapter 1 | 1 |
| 2. Chapter 2 | 9 |
| 3. Chapter Three | 16 |
| 4. Chapter Four | 21 |
| 5. Chapter Five | 27 |
| 6. Chapter Six | 34 |
| 7. Chapter Seven | 42 |
| 8. Chapter Eight | 46 |
| 9. Chapter Nine | 57 |
| 10. Chapter Ten | 63 |
| 11. Chapter Eleven | 72 |
| 12. Chapter Twelve | 80 |
| 13. Chapter Thirteen | 85 |
| 14. Chapter Fourteen | 92 |
| 15. Chapter Fifteen | 95 |

| | |
|---|---|
| 16. Chapter Sixteen | 101 |
| 17. Chapter Seventeen | 108 |
| 18. Chapter Eighteen | 113 |
| 19. Chapter Nineteen | 116 |
| 20. Chapter Twenty | 123 |
| 21. Chapter Twenty-one | 128 |
| 22. Chapter Twenty-Two | 136 |
| 23. Chapter Twenty-Three | 141 |
| 24. Chapter Twenty-Four | 147 |
| 25. Chapter Twenty-Five | 151 |
| 26. Final Chapter | 155 |
| 27. Epilogue | 159 |
| Also By MJ Ray | 162 |

# Prologue

6 Years earlier…

Harper

It can't be true. I'm sure when I wake up tomorrow, it will be a big misunderstanding. They're my mum and dad. How can they be splitting up? All the shouting and arguing, that's normal, surely, when you've been married so long. That's what people do. Splitting up is so drastic. I need to talk to Ed. He'll know what to do.

I check the time. Just after 5, he'll be home. I text him our code, the one that alerts him that I need him. Two words.

**Our Place.**

That's all I need to say. When I go to our den, he will be there.

My limbs are heavy as put my trainers on and make my way outside. This dark January evening is doing nothing for my mood.

Yeah, I need Edward. I get a thumbs-up back, so I know he'll be there. Mum and Dad won't notice I've gone. They're still talking in the living room. Our family meeting was over fast. It was, "Harper, we have something to tell you, but we don't want you to look at it as bad news." They seriously said that. How can it not be bad news? They went on to say they'll be happier apart, blah blah, so I'll be happier, and that I'll get to see them both, but not at the same time, and I get to decorate a new bedroom. Whoop. Who cares? I want my mum and dad to stay together. They're talking in the other room, but I can't make out anything they're saying. In case they realise I'm gone, I write a quick note on the kitchen wipe board "*Den with Ed.*" So they know where I am.

That's one thing they did right. My den. My safe haven where I spend most of my time. Dad made it for me when I was around seven, for me and the twin boys next door. Cooper and Edward. Thank god they moved in when I was six. Cooper is great, and yeah, I know him well, but Edward? I don't know what I'd do without my best friend. I know I will live my whole life and never find another best friend like him.

Now, five years later, I'm using the den more than ever. Ed and I spend most of our time there.

I walk through the back garden, down the winding path, taking in the different perfumes of the plants. If I close my eyes and breathe in, I can name all the plants in the garden – which I do right now so that my mind is on scents of nature and not Mum and Dad splitting up. I open the gate leading out of the garden, grab the waterproof torch that I hang on a hook at the side, and make my way into the woods. The leaves crunch under my feet, the frost setting in for the night. It's pitch black, but even without a torch, I'd find my way there. I get to the den and bend to get inside, reaching where the battery-operated lights are. There's a Minecraft torch, a lava lamp and a candle - things we've collected over the years to give us a little light. I sit on the makeshift floor, an old piece of lino covered with two blankets and two sleeping bags. We haven't slept out here for years, but the sleeping bags stay in here for extra comfort and warmth.

"It's me, Harp," Edward shouts from outside. Immediately my body relaxes and I unclench my jaw. He'll know what to do, what to say to make everything alright. Yes, I hero worship

Edward, but that's because he always sorts things out in that relaxed way of his. His presence calms me.

He pops his head through the den opening, his green eyes full of concern. "Hey, what's up?"

My tears come as soon as he gets the question out.

He pushes his way into the den, throwing himself down beside me. "Hey hey, it's OK, what's happened? Take a deep breath, Harp. Whatever it is, it can't be that bad."

"It… my mum and dad… they've just told me… it can't be real, Ed."

He puts his arm around me. "What can't?"

"They're getting a… a… divorce." I sob, not even sure he'll understand me in this state. I try to calm down, taking a deep breath.

"Oh my god, they're what? No… they can't be."

I nod. "It's true, I don't want to believe it, but they said that they've tried to make it work but decided they will be happier apart."

"Shit, Harp. That's awful."

"They said that they will make sure I'm OK, that it's nothing I've done blah, blah."

He is silent for a moment and exhales. "You've said that they argue, but I didn't realise it was this bad."

"Yeah." I whisper, "It's been horrible. They argue all the time."

He pulls me to his side. "Maybe it's for the best. Maybe they'll be happier apart. If they're not rowing all the time, maybe you'll be happier too."

I shake my head. This is too much to digest. "How will I get through this? I can't bear it, and what if I'm forced to stay with my dad and he's far away? What if I don't get to spend my spare time with you?"

"Nothing will stop us from being friends, don't worry about that. We will sort it. We own phones, if it comes to it, when you're at your dad's, we will video call, and maybe your dad will let me visit."

I take a breath in. Yeah, that sounds good. I'm sure Dad would do that. I nod, "I hope so."

"If they're not happy though, this might be for the best. I'm sure it feels awful right now, but give it a couple of days to sink in."

"I can't imagine ever being ok. Nothing will be the same again."

He squeezes my shoulder. "Trust me, you'll see. Your best bud is gonna help you through it, k?"

I sniffle and nod. "K."

And I know he will. Things will be tough, but I'll always have Ed.

Six months later…

I traipse down the high school corridor, hoping that I'm moving in the right direction. I check my map. It's horrible being new. High school is terrifying. It's noisy and busy. Everybody is so rough when they try to get past you, they shove you out of the way and its so hard trying to find out where your classes are. Luckily, my friend Heidi is in my form.

Travelling to school is fine because I get the bus with Edward and Cooper. They're in the year above me, but we all get on the same bus. The school arranged a smaller bus for a few of us that live the furthest from school. I don't see the twins much at school, but that's because they keep my year in a separate yard to help us settle in.

The twins being in the year above helps, though. They know everyone, and because I hang with them, everybody is super friendly to me. I love it when I walk into school with them. My protectors.

It didn't enter my head how much attention Edward and Cooper would get at school. Identical twins that are, *I guess*, good looking. I've never thought about them that way. They're tall, with brown hair and brown eyes... I guess they're hot. Cooper is just Cooper - he tolerates me, and we get on fine, but he likes to spend time on his own. Edward is my best friend. I can't imagine my life without him, but I've never thought of him as a *boy*. Watching these girls drool over him is kinda making me see him in a different light. Edward hangs around with the popular people, Cooper hangs around with a couple of guys who don't mix well with others.

I see how girls from their year judge me when I hang with the twins in their courtyard. They're wondering why an ordinary girl like me is hanging with the twins. They certainly don't see me as competition. All they do is look down their noses at me - the distaste rolls off them in waves. They are so intimidating.

When I'm in a higher year, I'll never look down on anybody the way they do. I could never be horrible and purposely hurt people's feelings. Edward is standing with a few of his friends so I walk over and lift my hand to tap him on the shoulder when what his friend says makes me freeze.

"Where's your hanger oner?"

"What are you talking about?" Ed asks his friend.

"The girl that keeps hanging around you, from year seven. She's punching above her weight if she thinks she's getting your attention. Why didn't you tell her to get lost?"

"Hey, that's my best friend you're talking about, so watch what you're saying."

Ed sounds angry. Good. Best friends stick up for each other. That friend of his is horrible.

"Oh, sorry man, that explains a lot. I didn't think she was your type. The girl next door type doesn't do it for me." His friend answers.

Edward laughs, relaxed now, "Nah, me neither. I like my girls to make an effort, girls that enjoy being feminine, not ones that constantly have dirt under their fingernails like Harper."

"Yeah, I get ya, but every guy prefers that, right?"

Edward shrugs, "I guess. I could never see Harper in that way. We were raised together. It'd be like fancying my brother."

His friend laughs, and they both walk off, oblivious that I heard every word.

Pain shoots through me as though a knife has been plunged into me. I don't see Edward in that light either, but I *do* see him as the most important person in my life, my person. My go-to for everything, every problem. The last couple of months have been hard. Dad moved out - it's been rough, and Edward is the one that's been there for me. I'd never have gotten through it if it wasn't for him and our time in the den. Every time I've had a wobble, he's been there, I think the absolute world of him, so for him to talk about me that way, it guts me. He was so dismissive of me. I mean, yeah, he defended me at the start of the conversation, but then he kind of laid into me. It hurts that he doesn't see me as a girl at all. I glance down at my uniform. It's the same as every other girl in the school. That's the deal with uniform - they want us all to appear the same. I look around at the other girls – their hair is styled instead of scraped back in a ponytail and they have perfect nails instead of dirt-ingrained nails. My obsession with flowers, gardening and different plants isn't kind on your hands - no matter how hard I scrub, I can't get them clean. Maybe I need to switch to gardening gloves. Some of the girls wear makeup—even though it's not allowed, they wear it in a way that they won't get in trouble—but it's there.

So that's what guys like… girlie girls who are into their appearance. That's what Edward likes. I thought he liked me, not in that way, but I thought he liked me as I am. I swallow to fight back the tears. The person I look up to most has said I'm not good enough for him.

His friends are laughing at me already, if they knew I was obsessed with gardening instead of makeup and hair? Perhaps I should keep that to myself. High school is rubbish. Why can't it just be Ed and me? Summer holidays in our den. I guess things need to change now I'm in high school - I guess *I'll* need to change.

# Chapter 1

Harper

Five years later…

The flyer catches my eye as I walk through the town centre;

**Do you have what it takes to create my garden of Eden?**

**Have the talent and the knowledge to make my garden into the garden of dreams?**

**This is an exciting opportunity to take part in a competition that will put your name on the map. My 15 acres needs you! I want originality. The garden of my dreams.**

**Interested?**

**Message the email address below and we will send you the schematics for the garden.**

**Prize? £50,000 plus a week in my four bedroomed villa in Portugal to be taken any time within a year. Flights included for six people.**

Wow. Bloody hell! Glancing around, making sure no one will recognise me, I take a picture of the flyer with my phone. I will check it out in more detail when I get home. I bite back a laugh. Anyone would think I was doing something illegal with how much secrecy there is around it. 16-year-old girls and gardening competitions don't go together. If anyone knew I was interested in this competition, it would seriously put my popularity in question. Still, £50,000 would massively help me out for Uni. Mum won't have the money to fund Uni the way things are at home.

Ah, I'll think about that later. Right now, I need to check that I'm perfect. I check the mirror app on my phone as I walk towards the Arndale, where I'm meeting the girls. Hair blown straight and then curled perfectly. Hidden makeup—light, eyelashes on, lips as plump as possible with my new gloss that, according to the wrapper, makes you look as though you've had filler and my eyebrows perfectly defined. Teeth, check, nothing in them and are white. I snap a selfie and post it on Instagram. #shoppingwithmygirls #manchesteralltheway. I put my phone back in my bag. I look good - good enough to blend in with the girls.

I check my outfit. It's a lovely spring day, so I went for my tailored light brown shorts with a cream check and a cream vest and wedges. Simple, but it actually took me an hour to pick it out to make sure it was just right and showed off my body in the right way. Being a girl is exhausting sometimes.

My phone rings. 'Ed calling'.

"Hey, what's up?"

"My phone is telling me you're in the city centre. What ya doing?"

"Stop stalking me! I'm meeting the girls. We're going shopping."

I can almost hear his eye roll. "So that will be four hours of your life spent in Primark that you'll never get back."

"Shut up. We're not only going to Primark. We're going to Top Shop, River Island, and having a coffee. It'll be fun."

Who am I trying to convince, him or me?

He sighs, "Yeah, whatever, have fun—it's not like you'd rather be knee-deep in the garden, right?"

I sigh but decide to ignore that comment - he doesn't get it. Image is everything when you're sixteen.

"We watching a film tonight?" I ask.

Silence at the other end of the phone.

"Ed?"

"I can't tonight. I'm busy."

I check for traffic as I cross into the busy pedestrianised area of Piccadilly gardens. "Oh yeah, what ya doin'?"

"Just a date." He says it so quietly that I'm unsure that I've heard him right.

"A *date?*"

He clears his throat. "Yeah, don't sound so shocked. Helen, a girl from my year, asked me out, so I thought, why not?"

Now it was my turn to be silent.

"You still there?"

I shake my head, "Er yeah, still here, OK, so I guess I'll see you tomorrow."

"Of course, we're going to Stanley Gardens, aren't we?"

"Yeah, if you still want to." *Why do I sound as though I'm sulking?*

"Harper, yes, of course I do."

"OK, tomorrow then."

I end the call. What the heck is that about? Edward going out with a girl. Thank god Heidi is coming with me shopping today - I can ask her opinion about this. I'll ask her before we meet Chelsea, though. Chelsea, the girl everyone hates, but the girl everyone wants on her side and to be her friend. It leaves a nasty taste in my mouth that I'm one of those people, but needs must. She is going for the most popular girl of the year award. Everyone wants to be around Chelsea. Everyone, unfortunately including me, is always so eager to please her. It makes me kinda sick and dislike myself a little, but it's worked for the last five years. You hang with the popular, you become popular - other girls leave you alone, and the guys notice you. It's a case of keep your friends close and your enemies closer.

The girls on the bus that I consider friends, Riley and Rosie, don't get why I hang with this gang. They say I'm too nice to be with these guys. That may be true, but I'll be in the sixth form and away from this drama in a few months. Anyway, I like attention. Dressing and acting this way gets attention. The trouble is, after five years of doing it, it's getting old.

I scan for Heidi. I want to sound her out about Ed.

Ed on a date.

Ed going out with a girl tonight, on a date.

Instead of spending it with me watching a movie or going to one of Connor's parties. It's fine, I guess—there's not much I can do about it.

It totally screws with the theory the bus gang had about him last month. They swore he had a thing for me. That they'd seen the way he looks at me, or whatever - obviously rubbish. I wish they hadn't said anything. It made things weird between us for a while, and how wrong were they? They should get their facts right. It made me analyse mine and Ed's relationship and doubt our friendship. Things have been weird, and Edward has no idea why. It's obvious now they were wrong.

"Harper!"

I see Heidi walking towards me. The others are meeting us there. I had to see my dad. He needed to spend his obligatory hour with me so he didn't feel guilty—he dropped me off here. Ah, the joys of having divorced parents - the need to make allocated time to see them. Heidi was bridesmaid dress shopping with her auntie.

"Hey, how's it going?" Heidi was wearing a short fitted pencil skirt and a vest top. Her brown bobbed hair was curled, and her glasses stylish and so on-trend. If she didn't need prescription glasses, I'm pretty sure she'd wear them anyway, as a fashion statement. She worked 'office chic' perfectly.

"It's going a little weird. The strangest thing has just happened with Ed…"

"Yeah? What? He didn't ask you out, did he?"

"*What*? Of course not. Why would you say that?"

She shakes her head and laughs. "I'm joking. What was weird about it?"

"He said he can't hang out tonight, that he has a date."

She frowns at me. "What's weird about that? He's a seventeen-year-old hot guy. I can't believe this hasn't happened before now."

I stare at her. "You think he's hot?"

"Your best friend is a hottie, and you know it. I could grab his face and snog it off." She motions, pursing her lips as though kissing and making smoochy sounds.

"Knock it off, and ew!"

"Sorry, I'm totally being serious now. Why is it bothering you? And *really* think about this before you answer."

Not sure what she's expecting me to say.

"Erm…I guess it's out of the blue."

She rolls her eyes. "Aw, you feeling neglected?"

"What no! Of course not. But I told you what the bus gang had told me. I knew it was rubbish—he doesn't see me in that way."

She grimaced. "I'm not sure about that."

I glance at her. "What do you mean?"

"It's hard to believe that a sixteen-year-old girl that looks like you do, and a seventeen-year-old guy that looks like he does, has nothing going on between them, or nothing has ever happened between them. It's weird. I mean, he's hot, tall, popular, funny. You've never even thought about it?"

I think back to being eleven when I believed that the sun rose and set with him. But did I ever like him that way? Maybe I would have if I hadn't had overheard him tell his friend that I disgusted him.

"No, nothing serious, kids' stuff. He doesn't see me that way. I'm not sure why it's bothering me so much that he has a date. I feel neglected or something. Silly because I have no right to his time, but how dare he!" I laugh.

She chuckles, "Who's he going out with?"

"Helen, she's in the sixth form with him. I clocked her talking to him last week. I don't know her, but she obviously has it bad for him - *she* asked *him*."

Heidi's eyes widen, "God, the girl has got guts. I can't ever imagine ever asking a guy out."

I shake my head. "No, me neither. Good on her, I guess. We'll see tomorrow if he's enjoyed it."

"I'm sure he will tell you all about it. Come on, we better not keep princess Chelsea waiting," Heidi sighs. She's not a fan, tolerating her only because of me.

I link her, and we head off to the Arndale together, ready to meet the others.

I spot them straight away at the Costa near the main entrance. Everyone is fawning over Chelsea. I sigh. I'm supposed to be over the moon that she and her friends decided to come with us today. Truth is, I can't stand her. I tolerate her because I've learnt to be popular, you have to put up with a few enemies on your team, whether you like them or not. Chelsea was a bitch to my friend Rosie over a guy, I mean, nasty. This is what I wanted, right? To be in the popular gang and fit in, so I better suck it up.

Chelsea spots us approaching and flicks her hair back. Someone with her personality being so gorgeous isn't fair – she should be ugly. Her auburn hair with blonde highlights is perfect, of course, no frizz in sight, big brown eyes that should be in a Disney movie, and slim enough to be a Victoria Secret model.

She narrows her eyes at us. "Girls, we thought you were never showing up." Her eyes drop to take in my outfit. I must pass because she says nothing. She does the same to Heidi, who must get a pass too.

"Chelsea, hey...hey everyone! We're not late, are we?" I put on my happy voice.

Chelsea shrugs, "It's fine. We're caffinated now, ready to shop. I need a killer dress for next Saturday night."

I frown, "Why? What's next Saturday?"

She waves her hand, "Connor's party, that's all, but a girl likes to look her best."

Hmmm, something going on there…

We go into every shop ever opened in Manchester. I buy a cute headband and a purse from River Island. Dad gave me £50.00 when he dropped me off, but that needs to last me a while.

I'm searching through the t-shirts in New Look when I overhear Tilly discussing a dress and trying to get Chelsea to buy it. "Come on, it's gorgeous. It will definitely catch his eye."

My ears prick up. My gossip meter has pinged. Has Chelsea got her eye on someone?

I go over to them. "Ooh, who do you like, Chelsea? Tell all."

She shrugs. "Well, there's someone I have my eye on. This dress will do the trick."

Truth is, she could wear anything and look good. That's what's so annoying.

"Whoever it is, he doesn't stand a chance. You always look good."

"Yeah, Edward will drool all over it." Tilly says.

I stiffen. Not my Edward? "What? Edward?"

Chelsea gives Tilly a look that I don't understand, and Tilly grimaces.

Chelsea regains her composure, "Yeah, I realise that you and him are friends or whatever, so I'd be grateful if you don't say anything. If I need your help, I'll ask for it, but I'm sure I'll be able to grab his attention all on my own."

Yeah, bet that's not all she wants to grab. What is it with Edward? Is every girl in the school after him? My skin prickles. I hate that girls are paying him so much attention now - don't they understand that he's mine? Not in the way they want him, but still...

Edward would never go for Chelsea, she's not nice and he's a good person. Although does a 17-year-old guy think logically? Or do they see a pretty girl with long legs, and their tongue rolls out and their eyes bug out like in a cartoon?

I realise she's waiting for a reply. "I won't say anything. Your secret is safe with me, but to keep you in the picture, he has a date tonight."

Her body stiffens. "Oh really? With who?"

I shrug. "Someone from sixth form."

She laughs and flicks her hair. "Ah well, whoever it is, it's not me. I'm not worried."

*Self-obsessed much?*

I'm now officially dreading the next party at Connor's. Having to watch Chelsea trying to get her claws into my best friend is not my idea of a good time.

I get home at eight. What will he be doing now on his date? I flop on my bed and switch on the next episode of Vampire Diaries. Damon and Stefan will distract me.

Why am I so possessive over him?

## Chapter 2

♥

Harper

"Come on, Harp, you must be ready by now." Edward whines from the bottom of the stairs.

I roll my eyes as I put on my lip gloss. "Come up. I'll be a minute."

"We have a train to catch."

"When have I ever been too late and missed a train or bus? Have faith, my friend."

He comes upstairs and leans on the door frame to my bedroom. I peer at him through the mirror while doing my lip gloss. He's wearing dark jeans, trainers, and a white t-shirt. He's getting so tall that his head is almost hitting the door frame. His hands are in his pockets with his feet crossed at the ankles. His hair is getting long now, so it curls around his ears, and his fringe has to be swept to one side so it doesn't go in his eyes.

"Harper, we have ten minutes to get to the station—stop messin' around."

I sigh dramatically. "Fine, I'm done… chill." I grab my bag, "Oh wait, I forgot to do a selfie."

He lifts his arms in frustration, "You are obsessed with selfies, do one on the train."

"But I can't say where I'm going."

"No one knows you're going to a gardening show on the train. You could be going somewhere cool - instead of dragging your bestie to a gardening show where everyone will be over sixty."

"I'm not forcing you to come." I snap.

He rolls his eyes, "I'm joking, come on."

Of course, I had no doubt, we make it to the train on time.

We get a seat with a table on the train, and I plug my phone in to charge. He hasn't mentioned last night. I bite my lip. Should I ask? Oh, sod it. "So, you gonna tell me about your hot date?"

He glances at me and then stares out of the window. "Yeah, it was OK."

"So, you like her?" I try to make my voice sound normal. Why do I have to try? It should be normal.

"Not like that, no."

"So, you won't be going out with her again?" My voice is quiet and hopeful. I don't want to share him with someone else. I already share him with his friends and basketball. That makes me sound super possessive, but its because we've always had each other, but since high school we're drifting further and further apart, not because of us, because of everyone else. I don't want things to change.

"No, why?" he raises his eyebrows at me.

I shake my head, trying not to let on that I'm secretly pleased. "No reason, just wondered."

What Chelsea said yesterday pops in my head. "Oh, you'll never guess what I found out yesterday."

He raises his eyebrows, "I thought you said you were going to stop gossiping, said you'd turned over a new leaf?"

He is mocking me, I try not to gossip, I do, and I could never be mean but I can't keep it in when I have information.

"Fine, I *won't* tell you who was buying a dress yesterday to impress you at the next party then."

I pretend to check my phone as though I've lost interest. There's no way he can resist asking me.

"Who?"

"You don't want to know, right?" I keep my voice light. God, I love winding him up.

"No, I do."

I put my phone away and look at him, "No, you *really* won't want to know." I laugh.

His face is blank.

"OK, promise not to let on that I told you?"

"I promise." He does a crossing his heart motion with his finger.

"OK, so I overheard Chelsea tell Tilly that she was gonna get your attention at Connor's next party."

His eyes widen. "What? Please tell me you're joking!"

I chuckle. "Why?"

"Because she is a She-bitch from hell, that's why!"

I laugh, "Well, better be careful, or she's gonna drag you down to hell with her."

He leans back in his seat, stares at the roof, and says, "Why me?" as though asking someone up there.

"It's your fault. You shouldn't be so attractive to teenage girls."

His eyes meet mine. "So you think I'm attractive, do you?" he waggles his eyebrows at me.

"*What?*" How the heck am I supposed to answer that?

"You're a teenage girl, right? Are you secretly pining over me and wishing I'd ask you out?"

My body and brain understand that he is joking, but my heart does not, and it picks up speed, followed by the blush rising over my chest and into my face.

"Shut up," I say, glancing down. *Please don't see me blushing.*

"Harper, are you going red because of lil'old me?"

"No, shut your face. Just 'cos a couple of girls have shown an interest in you, you suddenly think you're Harry Styles, get over yourself."

He bursts out laughing, "Jeez, Harp, relax, I'm kidding, still... funny to see your face."

He's silent for a moment before he says, "How am I going to get out of the Chelsea thing, though? I'll have to avoid her and hope she moves on to someone else."

I chuckle. He doesn't know her like I do. Once she sets her sights on someone, she doesn't stop until she gets a yes. Maybe she's met her match this time. He doesn't like Chelsea, so she may have her work cut out. Good, I don't want her messing with Edward. It's a win. He doesn't like her or the girl from last night, so all is good - things can go back to normal. I sigh with relief. Should I analyse why I'm so relieved? Probably, but I decide to bury it in the back of my mind.

*Real healthy, Harper.*

I grab my phone take a selfie to upload, and once I'm happy with the photo, I load it up. #trainride #teengirl #lazysunday and scroll through Instagram to see if anyone has posted anything - all quiet—and then Snapchat. I show him a clip from one of his friends, and we laugh at its stupidity, relaxing back into our usual banter.

"Oh, I've got something to show you." I scroll through my phone to find the photo I took of the flyer for the gardening competition. I hand him my phone. "What do you think of this?"

I let him read it, and after a second, he says, "This is great. You have got to do this, Harp. No question. You've done every garden in our street, and everyone wants you. You could win this. Do it."

"Yeah, I want to, designing my dream garden, how good would that be? It's my perfect dream competition. The size of the garden too, wow, and there's no budget—I could have free rein to do whatever I wanted, no holding back. It would be the best thing ever, but... I don't know."

He exhales and runs his hands through his hair, and glares at me. "This is ridiculous."

I shake my head, but before I get the chance to speak, he carries on, "No, Harper. You're excited about this, I can tell, yet you're thinking of not doing it, and I know why. Because you know you will win, and you don't want anyone to know that Harper Lloyd loves this stuff. You don't want people to think that you are anyone but a superficial girl into makeup and clothes. When are you going to get over this?"

I stare at my hands, "You don't get it, Cap." Captain is his nickname from when we were small. He was obsessed with Captain America and carried an old metal bin lid around for a shield - he painted it and everything - we still have it in the den. Back when things were simple. "Being popular is everything when you're a sixteen-year-old girl."

"You forget, I'm seventeen, and I don't think that way. I'm just me. People take me or leave me. If I have friends, great, but I've always got you. Why can't you be yourself? If people don't love you, which trust me they would, then you've still got me."

I shake my head. "It's not enough."

He leans back in his seat and stares straight ahead. "Great, thanks." He mumbles.

That wasn't supposed to sound so bad. I put my hand on his and squeeze. He looks down at our hands joined. "Ed, I didn't mean it that way. I meant I need to look and act a certain way if I want to fit in."

"Yeah, but that's what I don't get. Why can't you just be you? Because you are bloody amazing."

I turn my head to look at him, and our eyes meet. We don't say anything for a moment, looking at each other and then I sigh and rest my head on his shoulder. He slides his arm around me and draws me into him. "School is hard enough—I need my shield. We all like a shield, remember?"

He squeezes my arm. "Shut up. Why can't you be like this all the time, Cup?" He used to call me Buttercup because they were an obsession of mine, among other flowers, when we were small. As we got older, he realised 'Buttercup' sounds too much like a term of endearment, so he started shortening it to Cup, Cup and Cap. What a pair. We don't use these names much in front of others, but sometimes it slips out.

"You don't understand. Boys are attracted to girlie girls, right?"

He stiffens, "Please don't tell me that this is for guys' benefit?"

I shrug in his arms. "You telling me that guys don't like it when girls act that way?"

"Jesus, Harper, yeah, I am telling you that. Guys want you to be yourself, and why are you so bothered about guys, anyway? Do you have your eye on someone?" His voice sounds hard.

"No, in fact, I'm getting tired of the same old conversations with guys. Is it too much to ask that they see me as me? I've gotten so used to being this way that I don't know how to be anything else. I want someone to love me for me for a change."

Does he not know the lack of experience I have with guys? Sure, I flirt and smile in all the right places, but has Edward noticed that I've never been out with one? Never had a date.

Probably not. He's never said anything.

"I've built up this popular girl persona, and the only people I can be myself with is you, Cooper, and I guess the girls on the bus, to a certain degree."

"Trust me, plenty of people love you for being yourself, but you can't see it." He whispers.

I push myself away from him and sit straight in my chair "Anyway, enough self-pity from me. I'll think about it, and if I have the balls, I'll go for it."

He reaches and tucks a strand of hair behind my ear. His touch surprises me because we're not friends that show affection. I gasp as his touch leaves a warm feeling on my cheek. As his dark brown eyes meet mine, he gives me a sad smile, and the moment is over - life as I know it returns to normal, but I have to sit on my hand to stop myself from putting it to my cheek where he touched me.

Edward gets pulled around by me at the garden show. I get carried away telling him all about specific plants that he has no interest in whatsoever. Hey, I go to every basketball game for him, so this is his penance—although I do secretly love watching him play, but I'm not going to tell him that. In Edward's favour, he pretends he's interested and asks me questions. We have lunch and it's a great day. He was right though, we *are* the only ones there under sixty.

I'm going to do it. I need to be brave – and there's always a chance no one will find out, but if I don't enter this competition because of what people think, I'm an idiot. Decision made.

# Chapter Three

♥

Harper

I hate form time. It gives everyone too much freedom. Everyone chats about their weekend, and I do, too - pretending it was the most amazing ever. Thing is, it *was* good. I got to go to a gardening show, but I can't tell them that, so I rave about shopping and how awesome it was. Boring. Same old, same old. We talk about what we're going to wear to the next party.

Luckily, Chelsea isn't in my form, but a couple of her groupies are, so I have to behave suitably. They ask me how many likes I got on my Instagram post and how many followers I have—you know, proper life-altering stuff.

This form period is a win. My Instagram is winning me brownie points! Our form teacher is sitting at her desk, not taking any notice of us. She has put Newsround on the TV and is leaving us to it, as per usual.

She sits straight as though she's paying attention when the door opens, and our year head walks in. There is someone with her, a boy around our age, he's playing with his hands and can't look anyone in the eye, bless him, he's so nervous. He can't be a new boy…who starts school halfway through year eleven?

The year head, Miss Beeley, talks in a hushed voice to our form teacher and turns to speak to the class.

"Guys, can I have your attention. This here is Sam. He has had to transfer schools last minute and is now part of your form. I'm sure you can appreciate how hard it would be, to start a new school now in the last year, so please help him settle in."

He is average height and build with straight blonde hair, and his fringe is long and swept to one side. My heart goes out to him, God, how awful must this be.

Her eyes go around the class. "Let's see. Who hasn't done anything towards Curriculum For Life credit yet?"

CFL is a nothing lesson that is supposed to get us used to living in the real world, but it's good on our records for college or sixth form if we do good deeds. I need to do something—my something could be showing this guy around. I raise my hand and look around—I'm the only one with my hand raised.

"Harper, yes, perfect." She turns to Sam, "Harper will show you around and tell you everything you need to know."

"Harper, pack your things up, and you can start the tour."

I pack my bag and make my way over to him. I give him a big smile and he smiles back at me.

Miss Beeley looks at me. "You have lesson in form next, is that right?"

I nod, "Yeah, we have music together."

"Brilliant, I will tell your music teacher that you two will be late."

I shrug, "Sure, no problem." I turn to Sam, "Come on, let's get started."

We go to a huge school, so the tour might take a while. I don't mind missing music one little bit.

We leave the classroom and walk down the corridor. I turn to him. "How awful is this, having to start a new school in the last year?"

He rolls his eyes and flips his hair out of his eyes, "I know right, don't get me started. My brother moved here and brought me with him."

"Oh right." I wonder where his parents are.

He waves his hand, "Don't ask. It's a long story, one that involves lack of parents and brother needing to sell the house."

"Oh god, I won't, but it sounds like an awful story."

"Yeah, not the best. So, what's the school like?"

I shrug. "It's good, has its usual problems, but I guess they all do."

"Tell me about it. I seem to be a target for bullies."

He was softly spoken and quite effeminate. I'm guessing that's why he has gotten mean comments. People can be so hurtful, and high school kids? Most have no conscience!

"Well, you get any trouble, you come to me."

"You are gorgeous, aren't you?" He says.

I blush, laughing. "And already I love you! Come on, let's get you settled in."

I link him, smiling happily, knowing I've found a kindred spirit right here.

Sam is funny. We quiz each other on our lives as we walk around the corridors. I offered for him to sit with us at lunch and he was so grateful. He didn't come out and say he's gay, but I'm assuming he is, especially as we ran into Coop in the hall and Sam's jaw dropped. When I told him he was a twin, I swear he nearly passed out, so yeah, I'm pretty sure I'm right on that one.

Anna and Heidi follow Sam and me at lunch to grab a table. No doubt Chelsea and her group will pass by at some point, especially when they see I'm with the new guy. They will want all the details.

We take a seat, and I take a bite out of my panini. "So, how did it go this morning?" I ask Sam.

"Like a breeze, thanks to you." He turns to the girls. "How amazing is she? Gorgeous and the personality to match."

I roll my eyes but smile, "It's ok, Sam, you don't need to big me up to them. They already know I'm amazing."

Heidi's turn to roll her eyes, "Yeah, right."

We laugh, and there's a voice from behind. "What are you all laughing at?"

It's Ed. He takes a seat at our table and takes a massive bite of his sandwich. The sixth form has a common room where they eat, but sometimes he comes and has lunch with me.

I see Sam's eyes widen.

"We're laughing at how amazing Harp is."

He nearly spits out his sandwich, "Er, yeah, sure she is."

"Shut up. You obviously think I'm amazing. You're my best friend." I turn to Sam, "Sam, this is Edward, my best friend on a good day, my pain in the arse on another."

Sam smiles in a dream-like state at Ed. Yeah, definitely gay. "Er, hi, I saw another of you earlier."

Ed nods, used to the twin comments. "Yeah, I have a guy that is annoyingly going around with my face. I'm much cooler, though."

I chuckle. Cooper is way cooler than him.

"Nice to meet you. Hope everyone is being nice to you?"

Sam nods, "They are. I don't know why I was dreading it so much now. Everyone is so nice."

"Wait till you meet some of the others." Anna mutters.

Speak of the devil, I see Chelsea coming towards us. Wherever Ed is these days, Chelsea isn't far behind.

"Great," Ed mutters.

"Hey, everyone! Who is this? Aren't you going to introduce me?"

She walks to Edward, and luckily for her, but not so lucky for Ed, there's a seat empty. She sits and shimmies closer to Ed. She knows what she's doing.

"This is Sam. Sam, meet Chelsea." I say in between chewing.

"Hey Sam, where are you from?"

"I'm from Newcastle. My brother and I have just moved here." She frowns, "Your brother...where are your parents?"

Oh my god, like that's any of her business.

"Er, well, it's only my brother and me."

I decide to distract her. "So Chels, have you decided what you're wearing Saturday? I bet that purple dress you bought would be amazing with your colouring."

She is so easy to figure out—turning the attention to her always works. Sam shoots me a grateful look.

We get to hear the fine details of Chelsea's latest outfit and try our best to grin and nod where appropriate without falling asleep.

## Chapter Four

♥

Edward

I make my way down the halls of the main building as I say hi to practically everyone that passes. Our school basketball team is doing so well that everyone in school tried to cram into the gym for our last game, and I'm the leading scorer, so apparently, that makes me popular.

Popularity.

The thing that Harper is so obsessed with. Why she is like that, I have no idea. She never used to be like that in primary school. She changed when she started high school, turning into a different person when other people are around. Not mean - she could never be mean. Still, she surrounds herself with questionable personalities. I've noticed Chelsea has been hanging with her a lot. What is that about? Chelsea is horrible, and now that Harper has said she has her eye on me, well, that terrifies me. She may be gorgeous on the outside, but there is only acid on the inside - she corrodes everything she comes into contact with.

No game after school today, so I am on the bus with the gang. Chill out tonight - I'm aching from practice. A night in the den with Harper watching a film on her laptop sounds perfect. I have homework too, but who cares. I'll do that on the bus in the morning.

My apple watch buzzes, a message from Coop.

**Out tonight, tell Mum and Dad I'm hanging in the den with you.**

I frown. What is with him lately? He is being so secretive, even more so than usual, he's never been exactly chatty, but he's taking it to a whole new level recently. I should find out. The twin thing is usually damn good. We're completely different, even so, when he needs me, I kinda know and vice versa, so as much as he's being secretive, I don't need to worry. My twin senses would be tingling. I'll talk to him tomorrow.

I see Harper in the corridor and jog to catch her, that is until I realise Chelsea is with her—I slow down. Unfortunately, I catch Chelsea's eye when she looks over her shoulder, and she stops and turns around.

"Edward, I was just talking about you."

I raise my eyebrows and look at Harp questioningly. She gives me a slight shake of the head, barely there, but I saw it, I just don't understand what it means. You'd think I'd speak teenage girl by now, but no.

"Where are you going now?" I address Harper after giving Chelsea the minuscule of chin lifts.

"History, you've got Science."

I snort. She knows my timetable better than I do. "I know. See you on the bus."

She nods, and Chelsea tries to stop me as I walk past her. She grabs my arm. "You hanging at the park tonight?"

*Don't touch me, woman.*

"No, 'fraid not, Harp and I have plans, don't we?" I shoot a pleading look at Harper.

She nods. "Yeah, see you on the bus."

She links Chelsea and turns her away from me so that I can walk past her. The piranha has set her sights on me. Great. Little does she know that there's only one girl I want. Even if the chances of getting her are nil. You can't get more friend-zoned than the best friend. She doesn't even realise I'm a guy.

I shake my head as I run into my best friend, Jasper.

"What's the matter with you?" he says as he falls into step with me.

"Apparently Chelsea has a thing for me."

He laughs and pushes his glasses up his nose, "Give the rest of us a chance, eh?"

"Shut up. You totally have the nerd thing working for you, and you know it." He's the same height as me with short black hair and tortoiseshell glasses. The thing is, he wouldn't notice if a girl came right up to him and planted a smacker on him. Tech is what matters to him.

He shrugs, "Who has time for girls?"

I chuckle, yeah, he's a nerd, but I happen to know a couple of girls that are interested in him. He is more into gaming and coding or whatever the hell he does. He's a hundred times smarter than me.

"I'm not interested in Chelsea." I make a disgusted face.

"No, I know who you're interested in. Come on, let's get to class."

We head over to the science building, where we sit together.

"I wish I wasn't interested in Harp." He's the only one I've confided in about Harper. He was asking my advice on how to talk to girls, so I opened up to him. The looks Cooper has been giving me lately when I've been with Harper, though, I'm sure he knows. He'd never say anything to anyone - bro code.

"Dude, it's time to move on."

"Yeah, so you keep saying." He tells me at every opportunity that I'm wasting my time pining for Harper, that she's never going to realise I'm right in front of her face.

Jasper sighs. "I mean it, you can't keep doing this to yourself. Either tell her you have feelings for her or move on to someone else. Chelsea is into you, so you could distract yourself with her. Wait, you went on a date last week, right? So go out with her again. You need to move on."

I shake my head. "No way in a million years could I ever say something to her. It'd ruin our friendship. She's my best friend, Jasp, part of my life, my every day. No way can I lose that. And Helen, there was no spark. I told her we're better staying friends. Well, if a text counts."

He rolls his eyes, "So what about Chelsea?"

I shudder, "God no."

"So, your gonna carry on like this? Friend zoned for life?"

I sigh and run my hands through my hair. "If I could find out how she felt about me without actually telling her, I might know to move on."

He climbs onto a stool in the science lab and drums his hands on the table. "So why don't you… find out, I mean?"

"What? How?"

"Technology is a wonderful thing. Why don't you send her a message? Anonymously, be her admirer or some crap, you'd know if she was open to something, and no one knows her like you do, right? She might *see* you without *actually* seeing you - might fall for you, then you can turn around and tell her it's you, and she gets a two for the price of one package."

"That makes no sense."

He shakes his head, "I mean, if you talk to her about things you've noticed that other guys haven't, without her knowing it is you - maybe she'll fall for you, for your personality first or whatever. You don't stand a chance right now because she sees you as a mate - she doesn't see you as a guy." His eyes widen as though he's had a fantastic idea. "Wait, I've got it! You could do this, the secret admirer plan, win her over with your charms so that she's dying to meet this man of her dreams. In the meantime, you entertain as many girls as you can, right in front of her face. You've never bothered much with girls, you never give them a chance because of Harper, but if you show you're interested, she might see what the other girls see and that you're, well, I guess you're not *ugly*."

I snort, "Thanks, man."

"Come on, a few of the girls in sixth form are interested. All I hear about is Edward or Cooper. I know that you know but you don't entertain it, but what if you did? What if she saw you with other girls? Or in particular, Chelsea, because she's friends with her, so it would be right in front of her, she'd have to watch it play out."

He's so animated and excited.

Could this be a plan? Chelsea though? "I've got to say, I don't *hate* your idea, I mean, I'm sick of living like this - any bit of affection I get from her I wonder, could this be it, when she *really* sees me? But it never is. How would I do it, though? The email thing?"

"Get me her email address. I'll set up an anonymous email address, but one that won't go into her junk mail. I can do that. Important decision, though—name. You've got to get the name right. What do you want it to be?"

I shrug. "How the hell would I know?" What would catch her attention?

He taps his chin, looking into the distance, "What about something like Admirer101?"

"No, that sounds creepy and crappy." I get an idea. "What about *Rookiewithgirls*? That will show I'm shy or something, so I can't approach her face to face. Already I'll have her interest, cos she hates cocky guys."

He nods. "Yeah, let's go with that, although it's kind of misleading, isn't it? You're not a rookie."

I shrug. "You'd be surprised. I've never really entertained the idea of other girls."

"Yeah, but your best friend is a girl, so you understand teenage girls better than anyone."

I snort, "Yeah, right, my best friend since I was two years old has no idea I'm in love with her, and I have to do this to get her attention - rookie is right."

He chuckles and fiddles with his glasses again, a nervous habit he has. "OK, leave it with me. I'll text you when it's set up, I'll make it untraceable."

"Yeah, she's on the ball with technology. She lives on social media, so yeah, be careful."

"Oh my god, I need to set you up an Instagram, too - we can work this to our advantage. Leave it with me."

The teacher comes in as I roll my eyes, and we fall silent and get our books out. Is this the most stupid idea I've ever had? Maybe, maybe not. It could be that if she sees that someone likes her for who she is and sees through the superficial stuff, she'll believe it. She sure as hell doesn't believe it when I say it, maybe *Rookiewithgirls* can convince her. Anything is worth a go. I groan to myself. Do I *really* have to entertain Chelsea, though?

## Chapter Five

♥

Harper

*Hello Harper, I wanted to connect with you, and this was the easiest way I could think to do that. You see, I have a little crush on a certain beautiful girl around school - I'm not good with girls. It's taken me longer than it should have to pluck up the courage to send this email.*

*You are your own kind of beautiful. Inside and out.*

*I see you every day, so popular, so pretty, but there's more, I see the way you help people, the way you're there for your friends. I see **you**. Why can't everyone else see past the barrier like I can? Maybe they don't want to, or they're too tied up in their own lives. Who knows?*

*Sometimes you look so unhappy when you think no one is watching. Today in the lunch queue, I wanted to give you a hug, but that would have been so weird, right?*

*You are amazing. I wish you'd look my way.*

*Rookiewithgirls*

Sitting on my bed, I read the email again and again. Who could this be from? He saw me at school today. I bite my lip as I run through the list of guys in my year that I know. I cant think of anyone that would do this. Is it creepy or romantic? My instinct is saying kinda sweet. Whoever it is hasn't got the courage to talk to me face to face.

I reread it for clues. Someone that isn't good with girls. Someone that's had to pluck up courage to do this and sees me every day. God, that could be literally anyone. There are 250 kids in a year at school, and that's if he's even in my year. Excitement buzzes through me. I have a secret admirer! Should I email him back? What if he's disgusting? What if he has body odour and smelly breath...but what if he doesn't, and he's lovely? Or what if he's a weirdo? His email doesn't come across weird, though, he sees. Sees that I'm not being myself. My insides tense up. If he can see, can others see?

I check the time, 7pm. I grab my phone and message Edward.

**Usual.**

I drum my fingers as I wait for him to read it.

My phone buzzes with the 'thumbs up' emoji as I make my way to our den, picking up crisps and drinks on the way so that we can munch while we talk. Edward never stops eating, even though there isn't an ounce of fat on him, so not fair.

The den.

My favourite go-to place. Mine and Ed's place. Originally my dad built it for Ed, Coop and me when we were little, back when my dad was still my dad. My heart twists as I remember how it felt to have my dad around all the time. We laughed so much back then. Now my mum and I just pass each other on the way out. She works so much as a staff nurse at the hospital or, more recently, out on a date. She has started to date again, and I'm not sure I like it. I know she has to move on, of course, it's been years, but there's a different guy every week, and they all seem like total a-holes. None of them are nice, and she fawns over them and goes over the top with how she looks, spending hours getting ready for them. So yeah, Mum and I are not in a good place anymore.

Dad built my den with old 4 x 4 when he was re-doing the decking in the back garden. Living next door to Ed and Coop means that we've hung out in each other's houses a lot, and Ed and I, we hit it off from day one. We used to build dens in the back garden and sit in them for hours.

Behind our houses, there's a patch of trees. It's not a big space, a quarter of a mile by a half a mile – it belongs to the row of our houses. When we were old enough to be trusted, we played in there - we *may* have got lost a few times, but we always found our way back. It's spending time there that began my love of nature and plant life. Sitting in there and listening to the natural sounds around you. Heaven. After seeing our love of den building in the back garden, Dad used the old decking and built us a hut, or a den as we still call it, even though we're not eight anymore! It's the size of a small storage shed and is built around an old tree. Dad used the tree as a girder for support. It's pretty low, needing us to crouch as we go inside. Edward can't stand upright in it anymore.

I get to the den after him, and he's already switched on the battery-operated lights and torch. We have it kitted out how we wanted. It's the comfiest place, with blankets and sleeping bags. Dad even laid boards for flooring. There are no windows, but we have pictures all around.

"We need to tidy in here." He says to me as I get inside.

There is litter scattered around and empty bottles of coke and sprite. Yeah, he's right, it needs a sprite and clean.

I scrunch my nose, "Yeah, let's have a cleaning session tomorrow after school."

He groans, "Ah, I didn't mean that I wanted to do it."

"Yeah, you wanted *me* to do it. Tough, we'll both sort it out, make it comfy again. I'll take the sleeping bags home with me and shove them in the wash."

He nods and sighs. "Fine. What's up, Buttercup?" he leans back on the sleeping bags, stretching out. He is the length of the den now. It's crazy that this place used to be huge to us - our very own house, and now we can barely fit.

I roll my eyes at my nickname. Part of me likes it, part of me hates it.

"You won't believe what's just happened."

I tell him about the email and what it said. "Hmmmm, I bet it's Peter Davies, the guy who always has food in his teeth and has personal space issues."

*Oh god.* "Shut up!"

"Or it's Abraham. How much of a match would you be with Abraham?"

Abraham is the loudest and most annoying guy in our year, always in trouble, but for some reason, extremely popular. He *has* been trying to talk to me a lot lately.

"Oh no, it cant be, can it? He has been paying me a little special attention."

Ed straightens, frowning. "Has he?"

"Yeah, can you imagine? But what if it is him? What if he's not like that on the inside? Maybe the loud exterior is a front, what if inside he's sensitive?" I wonder... he is good looking.

And he relaxes back and laughs. "It can't be him. The admirer guy says he's inexperienced with girls, and Abraham has been out with half the girls in the school."

I nod. "True."

Hmmmm. "Should I message back?"

He shrugs. "Up to you. Are you interested in finding out who it is?"

"I mean, yeah, he says he's not only interested in me because of how I look, that he's seen that I'm a nice person, so that shows he's not superficial. He might be nice. I hate that he knows who I am, but I don't have a clue who he is. Argh, I don't know. I'll leave it for now. I'm not sure what to write back. 'Thank you for your email.' What am I? A businesswoman? I'll see if he messages again. It's exciting, though, isn't it?"

He shrugs but doesn't look at me. "I guess."

We have a cushioned floor lined with carpet that used to be in our living room. The wood is bare, and we can see the branches through the gaps in the wood, but it is waterproof. Dad lined it with Perspex so we could see out through the top, but nothing gets in. It also keeps the creepy crawlies out. I don't mind bugs, if you're into gardening, you have to get past the bugs, but I don't want them in here with me.

I lie back and look around. Our history. Pictures we've painted or drawn are scattered on the walls, stuck on with blue tack and tacky ornaments that we've collected from holidays in the past. Ed and Coop's Mum and Dad, Pete and Carrie, have a summer house in the Lake District. They're like my second mum and dad. Ever since my dad left, I've been with them to the lake house. It's right by Ullswater lake with the most breathtaking views. The prettiest and most relaxing place on earth. Every time we've been there, we've collected things… pebbles, gnarled wood, pinecones, stuff like that, they're scattered everywhere too. It needs a clear out. The problem is I love these things, they're my childhood and Ed's. Still, a bit of order might be nice.

He lies back and places his hands behind his head. His t-shirt rides up and I get a glimpse of his toned stomach. I try to look away - I mean - it's Ed. But he is so toned. My hormones must be going crazy at the minute because this is Ed we're talking about. I shake my head and drag my eyes away.

"What does your ideal guy look like?" he asks, out of the blue.

I frown. "What do you mean?"

"If you could describe your dream guy, what would it be?"

*Hmmm, what would it be?*

"I guess someone that makes me laugh."

"Go on…"

"Someone taller than me. I like tall guys. Oh, and someone that sends me a text in the morning, something cheesy like 'good morning gorgeous', so you know you're on his mind. Knowing you're on someone's mind first thing in the morning would put a smile on your face all day, wouldn't it?"

"I guess," Ed says quietly.

"What's your ideal girl?"

He frowns. "Um, someone that I find easy to be around, gorgeous of course and, I guess kind-hearted."

"And big boobs, right?"

He bursts out laughing, "You know, us guys, we don't care about the size, you've got them, we're interested."

I roll my eyes. I believe him. Even being average build in that department, I've still noticed some guys can't look you in the face while you're talking - they're too interested in what's going on a few inches lower.

I laugh and lie beside him and rest my head in the crook of his arm.

"It'd be nice to have a boyfriend, someone to share everything with - like I do with you, but with the added benefit of kissing."

He's quiet for a moment before muttering, "Yeah, that'd be nice."

"Do you think we'll get that? It's weird to imagine us not being able to do this."

"Why wouldn't we be able to do this?"

"Probably because a guy wouldnt like it, or a girl, if you started seeing someone."

He sighs, "I suppose not."

"What are you doing now? You wanna watch a movie?"

"Sure, but it's my pick."

I sigh, "Fine."

I nip home to grab my laptop. Mum is working the night shift at the hospital tonight, so I'm free to do what I want.

He picks *The Fast and the Furious*. We started from the first in the series a couple of weeks ago, we're on the fourth now. I check my Instagram and find nothing new there, so I settle to watch the movie with my bestie.

I wake with something warm and cosy around me, a great big blanket. I snuggle deeper into it until the blanket moves, almost as though... yes, almost as though it's breathing! Sitting quickly, I shake my head. Where am I? Looking around, I expect to see the lilac walls of my bedroom. Instead, I see wood and smell grass and trees. Oh god. The blanket I've been lying on is Edward! I shake him. "Ed! Cap! You need to get up, now!"

He moves and grunts. I shake him again. "Ed, up now!"

His eyelids flutter open, and in my half-asleep panicked state, I can't help but notice how cute he looks.

"What the hell?" he says, but I see the moment it dawns on him that we fell asleep together in here. I check my phone - 6 am! "Ed, your mum and dad are going to kill us. We need to do damage limitation - they might still be in bed - you could sneak in."

"They're gonna know we only fell asleep in here—no big deal."

"So, you're telling me a sixteen-year-old and a seventeen-year-old boy sleep together all night, and they're gonna believe it was totally innocent?" My voice is getting more and more high pitched.

"But it is innocent!" he says, his voice still gruff from sleep.

"Yeah, well we know that but come on, if you were our parents, would you believe it?"

He gives a short laugh. "Jeez, Harp, relax. Your mum is on nights, and my mum and dad will still be in bed. Let's go back. No one will know."

I hope to God he's right. If his mum and dad stopped us from seeing each other, I don't know what we'd do.

## Chapter Six

Harper

We got away with it, not that there was anything to get away with as such, but yeah, his mum and dad were none the wiser. I've got to admit, though, it concerned me how nice it was sleeping with him. He was so comfy and safe and warm. Can't believe I've slept with a boy - even though it was Ed and he doesn't count.

Anticipation floods my body as I walk into school grounds. I had another email this morning, around an hour ago.

*Morning, Beautiful. I hope it's OK to message you again. Today, in one of your lessons, I*

*will leave a white rose, when you see it, know that I'm thinking about you.*

I mean, seriously, how romantic is that? It's like something out of a film. Do these things actually happen? Who could it be? I suspect everyone as I walk into school, eyeing them, wondering if it's him. I need to get a physical description out of him, even a vague one would do.

Edward turns to me and leans to speak low in my ear, "Wonder what the gossips would say if they knew we spent the night together?"

I gasp, "Behave! What if someone hears you?"

He laughs, "Lighten up - it was a joke."

"Yeah, but if anyone finds out, I'll get a reputation."

"What about me?" He places his hand on his chest and then slides his arm around my shoulders, "Relax, no one will know, K? My lips are sealed. Was kinda nice though, right?"

He gives me a lopsides grin. I'm not sure how to answer, but the truth is, yeah, it *was* nice.

I shrug, "Of course, you get to wake next to this…" I gesture to myself. Keeping it light is the way to go.

I look ahead, and my heart sinks as I see Chelsea walking our way. Crap. I'm not in the mood for her. Right Harper, put on your "I want to be accepted at school" image and get on with it. I plaster a smile on my face. "Hey, Chelsea."

Her eyes are on Edward as though he is a carton of ice cream.

"What? Oh, hey." She turns to Edward, "Hey you, how's it going?"

I smile to myself, waiting for him to brush her off. My mouth drops open when he smiles at her, as though he's happy to be her ice cream!

"Hey Chelsea, how's it going? You wanna walk with us?"

I nearly stumble over my feet. Why is he being nice to her? I mean, apart from the obvious - that she's stunning.

Her eyes light up, "I'd love to." She shifts direction to walk with us and links her arm through his. Now, that isn't much, but HOW DARE SHE! What is she doing? Total proprietary move. She casts a sidewards glance at me. Yeah cow, I saw it. The thing is, Edward doesn't seem to mind, he's totally enjoying it, which aggravates me even more.

Ed has form period at the other side of school, so I expect him to split off from us when the bell goes, but he doesn't. He turns to me. "Harp, can I have a second with Chelsea?"

The expression on her face makes me want to punch it. My hands curl into fists. She thinks she's won the lottery. We're usually inseparable and what is this interest in girls suddenly? It makes my skin prickle. I don't like it.

Whatever... leave them to it. "Sure, I'll see you later." I walk off wondering what the heck just happened, but suddenly remember my secret admirer! He's leaving me a rose somewhere. My step gets a spring in it as I walk to form.

OK, where is the stinking rose? I have gone through school all day searching for it... nothing. Maths is my last lesson, great... not my strongest subject.

I sit at my usual desk and get my book out. Tonight, I'm going to draw plans for my garden for the competition. Plus, I might do a couple of Instagram posts. I have around two thousand followers. A lot are from school - working at popularity is hard.

I send Edward a quick text while the teacher isn't paying attention. **You on the bus?**

**No, at practice.**

Oh yeah, Wednesday. **Want company? I can come and watch.**

He reads it straight away but doesn't answer. I get a reply ten minutes later. **It's OK, Chelsea is coming to watch me**.

What. The. Hell?. *What is happening?*

I reply; **OK, where is Edward? You have snatched his body and took up host. Where is the real Edward?**

**E; What do you mean?**

**Me; You're not into Chelsea!**

**E; Says who?**

He can't be serious. **Er, you?**

**She's not so bad. We've been getting along lately.**

I frown at my phone. Is he for real? Fine, he's obviously thinking with his eyes and what he can see rather than his head and soul.

**OK, fine, I'll catch up with you later.**
**You being stroppy?**
**No, I'll speak to you later, enjoy practice.**

If I could spit out a text, I would have.

"**K**" is all I get back. Fine. Have it his way. I have other friends.

I glance at the board as the teacher walks in, and my mouth goes dry. On the board in chalk is the most perfect drawing of a rose I have ever seen. It's so detailed and stunning and coloured lightly in white. My white rose. All there is at the bottom is a dash and the letter C. Letter C? Now I have to go through every boy I know beginning with C. It's a big school, and I don't know everyone - even though I try. What are my chances of finding this guy?

I nearly shout out for Mrs Madden to stop when she wipes the board. There goes my rose—but not before I got a sneaky picture of it with my phone.

At the end of school, I get on the bus with Rosie and Riley. Rosie is new and totally gorgeous. She caught the eye of Liam, who is on the basketball team with Ed and resident bad boy, or reformed one - now those two are an item he's been on his best behaviour and they are inseparable. She's without him right now because he's at training with Ed.

Riley is my sport obsessed friend. She will make it to the Olympics one day. After a terrible injury, she picked herself up and swapped from Gymnastics to Swimming, and she wins every race. I have never met anyone as competitive as her. She recently caught the eye of Rosie's brother, which was a surprise as he's older, at Uni, but they fell for each other - love is in the air - for everyone but me.

"Hey Harper, you seem depressed. What's up?" Riley asks.

"Nothing. Well… something… but it sounds pathetic."

Rosie turns to me. "That's fine, we can take it. Why do you look as though you just stepped on a butterfly?"

"You won't believe it. I've been binned off by Ed, for, get this, Chelsea!"

"What?" Rosie gasps. She dislikes Chelsea—big time—all the girls at our school do. When Liam showed an interest in Rosie, Chelsea got jealous and tried to get her claws into Liam many times. She tried to stir a lot of trouble between them, and she was mean and insulting to her.

"I always watch him at basketball practice. He said he arranged for Chelsea to go and said, I quote, *'she isn't that bad.'* Is he blind *and* deaf? Actually, scrub that, his eyesight is working fine—that seems to be what he's thinking with—she's nice to look at. I bet he can't wait to have her watch him at basketball, impressing the guys. Urgh, stupid boys."

"He is out of his mind. Why can't he pick a nice girl?" Rosie says.

"Why the sudden interest in girls, anyway? He's never bothered before." I ask them.

They both glance at each other.

"What?"

"Could it be, possibly, that you are jealous?" Rosie asks and winces as though she's scared to ask.

"*Are you crazy*? Why would I be jealous?"

"Well, she's stealing your guy's time." Riley says.

"He's not my guy in that way." God, I sound pathetic.

"Well, no, but you're used to spending time with him."

I shake my head. "Maybe…Jeez, I don't know. I hate it - I hate the thought of him being happy that she's there watching him - it leaves a bad taste in my mouth. It makes me boiling mad even though I have no reason to be mad. Bloody hell!"

"Aw, sorry hun, I get you. Listen, we're going to hang at the Trafford Centre tonight. We're getting the bus there, and Russ is picking us up." Riley is happy and loved up. If her pupils turned into love hearts, I wouldn't be surprised, but hey, I'm bitter. "Why don't you come with us?"

I sigh. "I'd love to, but I've got homework to do and Instagram stuff."

Riley waves her hand in front of my face. "Hello, you realise that's not compulsory, right? Well, the homework maybe, but the social media stuff? Sack it off."

I shouldn't, but I've never felt less like doing social media stuff than I do right now.

"You know what? Sod it, I'm gonna come. I don't want to be on my own tonight. If Edward can move on, so can I."

"Yey! What do you think about *Five Guys* for dinner?"

I nod. "Sounds good. Sign me up."

"This is just what I needed guys, thanks so much." I juggle my bags, happy with my purchases. "It's so much fun hanging with you guys."

Rosie smiles at me, "Yeah, you should do it more often."

Maybe I should. It's fun not having to constantly wonder what they think of me or what I should say or do before I say or do it. It's relaxed. How it should be. But while Rosie and Riley aren't exactly unpopular, they aren't in the same group as me. Liam, Rosie's boyfriend, is popular, but he fell into it the same as Edward. It's easier for guys, they're good at sport they automatically fit in. Me, I have to work for it.

Each one of us has a satisfying number of bags to carry. When we can't shop anymore, we head over to five guys. Rosie has booked a table.

The orient is a humongous space housing the restaurants. It's set out to imitate the bow of a ship - a big cruise-liner. It has a pool in the middle, for decoration only, a big TV screen and lots of tables in the middle with eateries all the way around. 'Five Guys' is one of them.

As we head over, I recognise a group of guys from school sitting at a table. I see Abraham and fleetingly wonder if he could be my admirer.

I messaged him after I saw my rose,

*It is beautiful. I love it. Unfortunately, it has been wiped from existence now, but I got a*

*picture first.*

I attached the picture.

*So, your name begins with C?*

I got one back five minutes later,

*Glad you liked it. My name begins with C, maybe? More of the same tomorrow, Beautiful.*

That's all it said, so I wonder what I'll find at school tomorrow? It's exciting and takes my mind of Edward. Distraction technique seems to be working.

The server takes us to our seat, and it turns out to be right next to the guys. Abraham watches me walk towards them. I give him a small smile, just in case, he raises his eyebrows in surprise. I rarely give him the time of day.

"Hey, Harper." He says as I near him.

"Hiya," I say as I sit with the girls.

The guys must have been here for as long as we have as their food comes at the same time as ours.

Once we're done eating the best burger in the world, even though I paid twelve pounds for it, Abraham comes over and sits beside me in the empty seat.

He points at my bags, "So you've been shopping?"

I try not to groan at his obvious question. "Yeah, you?"

"Nah, hanging here for somewhere to go."

I nod.

I glance at Rosie and Riley, and they're both trying to fight a grin.

"Harper, I was wondering if you'd like to... maybe do something with me one night?"

I bite my lip. He's a good-looking guy, but I don't feel attracted to him. Maybe because I hardly know him, I'm not sure, should I give him a chance? What if he is *Rookiewithgirls?* The name doesn't fit, but it could be him - he might be this sensitive guy deep down. I've always judged him from the surface. Maybe I should try to get to know him.

I nod. "Sure, why not? I'd like that."

He looks so shocked I nearly laugh. "Cool, can I have your number? We can arrange it."

I nod and hold my hand out, "Give me your phone."

He does as I ask, and I program my number into his phone.

I hand it back to him, "There you go, so we can maybe meet up."

He nods, "Yeah I'll make sure we do, thanks Harper, I best get back to the guys, have a nice rest of the evening."

That went well. He's already nicer than I thought he was. Maybe I should give him a chance.

It's late when I get home, but I begin my design for the garden. I lose myself in the design and research plants and what works well in direct sunlight, excitement bubbles in me as I design - I'm beginning to believe what Edward and my mum is saying - I have a knack for this stuff.

My phone lights up, a text from Ed; **usual**

Weird, why does he want me?

It's almost 10, not sure what Mum will say about me going to the den now. I message him the thumbs up and go downstairs.

"Mum Ed wants me for something at the den—I won't be long."

"It's late, Harper. What does he want?"

I shrug, "I'm not sure, but he wouldn't ask if he didn't need me to go. I'll be thirty minutes, tops."

She sighs, "Fine, you've got half an hour."

I nod, "Ok."

I make my way out, grabbing my torch on the way.

## Chapter Seven

♥

Edward

I put my phone down and wait for her, dread clutching at my stomach - this will not go well.

She's already pissed off with me. The plan is working—the one where she sees me with other girls. All I seem to do is aggravate her and push her away. But if Jasper is right, and this is what I have to do to make her jealous, then I have to go with it. If all she ever sees me as is her friend, then I guess I'll know soon enough.

I got a message as *Rookiewithgirls* from her earlier while I was at practice. It read;

*I loved my rose. It was something beautiful to brighten my ugly day.*

Why did she have a horrible day? Was it because of me? My stomach clenches at the thought of her having an awful day because of me. This is hard. I want to make her happy all the time, want to see her smile. God, last night though, I can't believe we fell asleep together. That was a close one. How understanding are parents supposed to be? They trust us, but that will only go so far. Her body next to mine, though... I love her. I love her so much, but Jasper is right, I can't keep on like this. The need to know is overtaking everything else, but I'm terrified.

She doesn't see me in that way, though - I could end up screwing up everything. I know what I have to do, but it's going to kill me to carry it out. She's mine, and I'm hers. Am I going to mess with that? She could hate me—it's for the right reasons, though... right? Don't they say there's a fine line between love and hate? I need to force a reaction out of her one way or another.

I hear the crunching of the leaves and twigs outside. She's here.

*Deep breath, you can do this.*

She steps inside and my breath hitches. Why does she always look so perfect? Her blonde hair is flowing down and loose and, well, messy. She's in her pyjamas and has an oversized thick chunky cardigan to keep her warm. This should not equal perfection, but it does. She's perfect for me. She sits next to me. "Hey, stranger." She sounds sad.

"Hey, sorry about before, about basketball practice."

"It's OK, I get it. You're into Chelsea."

I shrug. My mouth is dry – if I tell her I am, I'd be lying. "That's why I wanted to talk to you. I want to clear the air."

She raises her eyebrows. "Yeah? Have you come to your senses?" she's biting her lip. She always does that when she's stressed.

"Don't be like that."

"Sorry, what am I thinking...she's *exactly* the type of girl you're attracted to, right? Up her own arse, thinks the world owes her a favour, constantly wanting to win a popularity contest."

*Wow, Harper, Chill.*

I raise my eyebrows at her, "You'd know a bit about that, right?"

"Don't go there, Ed."

I shake my head. This is not how this conversation was supposed to go. "Sorry... I wanted to explain that I've decided to see where things go with Chelsea. I mean, she *is* your friend, right? You talk about her as though you hate her guts, yet you hang around with her all the time."

Harper stays silent but glares at me. What is she thinking?

"Yes, she's my friend." She spits the words out as though nothing is further from the truth.

"So, you won't mind if I see her out of school, hang out with her…"

I search for a sign - any sign at all that she cares.

She shrugs, "Go ahead. You're free to do what you want."

"Yeah, I am." My heart explodes into a million pieces. I hold her gaze. "Thing is, I don't think she or any girl would be too keen on going out with a guy that spends so much time with a girl, especially a gorgeous one like you."

Something flashes in her eyes, but I can't read it. God! You think I'd know this girl better by now… I know nothing! I don't think I'll ever understand how a girl's mind works.

"So, you're saying that we can't be friends anymore?" Her voice is shaky, but I don't think it's with fear, it's with anger. *Oh crap.*

"No, of course that's not what I'm saying."

She narrows her eyes at me. "Has Chelsea told you to do this?"

I shake my head. "No, I've decided to do this. I'm not saying I can't hang out with you, Harp, just not so much. We hang out all the time."

She stands and leans forward. "I'll tell you what, I'll make this really simple for you. You don't have to speak to me at all, how's that? I'd hate to cramp your style."

I sigh and run my hands through my hair. "Stop acting like such a baby."

"Piss off, Edward. You've seen something pretty and shiny, and you want it, and you don't care who you hurt while you go about getting it."

"You're blowing this way out of proportion. I'm not saying we can't see each other, but we need to tone down how much time we spend together."

She shrugs, "No skin of my nose. Do what you want, but don't expect me to be there when you get bored."

She goes to leave. "Don't leave it like this, Harp. I hate it when we fall out."

"Well, stop being an idiot."

She leaves, and I collapse back onto the sleeping bag. *Shit. That went totally wrong.* I wanted her to be annoyed or jealous, but I did not expect her to fall out with me altogether.

I grab my phone and compose a message from *Rookiewithgirls;*

*Hey gorgeous girl.*

*Hope your day is going better today, don't let people get you down - sometimes people have things going on in their own lives and don't realise what they're doing to others. I didn't have a great day today, but at least the thought of you smiling at my*

*rose made me happy. I enjoy drawing - it's something I do when I'm stressed—I've never done it to impress a pretty lady. It worked, right? It impressed you? I hope so.*

*Tomorrow, you will find sweetness everywhere.*

I have a plan for tomorrow that will make her smile, her best friend may have upset her, but her secret admirer will cheer her up.

## Chapter Eight

♥

Harper

I've been to a hundred (or it feels like) of these parties, but this one is strange because I haven't walked in with Edward. We've always gone to Conor's parties together, we live right next door to each other - we always travel places together - but not tonight, tonight I've come with Heidi nd Anna, and Edward? He has come with, yup, Chelsea. I can't believe it. I was still hoping that it was some sort of joke. But no, here he is with Chelsea.

It's as though I've lost an arm these last couple of days because I haven't been hanging out with Ed. It doesn't help that so many kids are asking, 'Where's Ed?' 'Why aren't you with Ed?' It's driving me crazy. I don't want to tell anyone that we've fallen out. It sounds so childish. It *is* childish.

I keep replaying the argument in my head. Was I being irrational? Why was I so mad about him and Chelsea? Every time I think about them together, my blood boils. I hate it. Did I overreact? God, I don't know.

Thankfully, my admirer has been keeping me busy. He messaged me the night I fell out with Ed and told me he'd make the next day sweet for me. Every lesson I went into, there was a sweet or a lollipop waiting on my desk. He must have found out what my lessons were and gone in before me to sneak a sweet on my desk. How was he not seen? There was only one lesson he couldn't do, and that was music. The room is always locked because of the expensive equipment - so he doubled up on the sweets in geography - the lesson before Music - with a note; '*Double the sweetness because the music room doesn't care about me impressing a pretty girl.*' That one made me laugh, so he's not perfect. He can't get around everything. Who is this guy? I asked him to describe himself last night, and he wouldn't tell me what year he was in said he was tall with brown hair and brown eyes. It doesn't rule out many, but he said he was popular, which makes me think more and more that it could be Abraham. He's tall with brown hair and eyes, plus he's popular. He hasn't messaged me yet from taking my phone number in the week, but he might be here tonight.

Anna leans in to me as we walk up the path, "I'll give you the nod if I see them."

I sigh. "OK, I want to avoid seeing them together—throwing up everywhere might be embarrassing."

Heidi chuckles, "I'm gonna tell Chelsea you said that." She's joking... I hope!

I narrow my eyes at her. "Don't you dare. Are you trying to get me in the popularity dungeon?"

"We promise we will say hello now and again."

They're joking. They're good guys. It's the rest of them I don't trust. They were as stunned as me when I told them what Edward had said.

Anna motions towards my outfit. "Well, you don't look as though you're suffering, losing your partner in crime. In fact, I have never seen you look so gorgeous."

Gorgeous. Edward said I was gorgeous. Why did I like that so much?

"Thanks babe, thought I'd go all out - my secret admirer said he'd be here tonight, and I'm guessing Abraham might be. Is it the same guy? I'm on the lookout for a tall guy with brown hair, brown eyes, who says he's popular, oh, and his name begins with C. Abraham isn't C, but maybe a middle name?"

"Hmmm, think we need to do some detective work, eh Anna?" Heidi asks her.

Anna nods, "Absolutely. Ed isn't the only one that can get a date, right Harp?"

Oh god, that makes me sound so pathetic. The truth is, I *am* jealous. I hate not being his only person. He has other people in his life. What the hell is that about? It should be me and me only.

I don't get it. "What is it with Ed, anyway? Why are girls fawning over him all of a sudden?"

Heidi and Anna exchange glances.

"What?" I ask, looking between them both.

"Well…" Heidi starts, "we were talking about your secret admirer, but you're still on Ed. And by the way, are you serious? He's gorgeous. Him and his brother are the hottest guys in school, but while Cooper is unapproachable, Ed isn't - he's one of the nicest guys ever. That hair… how it flops in his face, and when he smiles, those dimples… seriously gorgeous."

They think he's gorgeous. Why does this make me suddenly want to slap my friend?

*Get a grip, Harper. He's not yours to own.*

Anna speaks, "You can't tell me that you don't think he's gorgeous. I don't care how long you two have been friends, Jesus, you have eyes, right? His smile, it's so warm as though he thinks you're the only girl in the world, sometimes I wonder if he realises he's flirting or just being himself, either way, it's hot, everything about him is hot."

I've never studied him objectively, but I guess they're right. That lanky ten-year-old has turned into a hottie and one all the girls fancy.

"Has nothing ever happened between you two, ever?" Heidi asks incredulously.

I shake my head, "No. I had a bit of a crush on him once when I was around eleven, but…"

"But what?"

Both of them look at me wide-eyed, waiting for the next instalment of the story.

"Nothing, come on."

"Tell us."

"No, it doesn't matter, come on, let's get this party started."

It's only a matter of time before I see them. My stomach clenches when I see them together. They seem cosy - standing close to each other, talking, I watch them for a moment. I hate it. I hate watching him be friendly with her. She laughs at something he said as though he's the funniest guy on earth. *OK honey, he's not that funny*. Who am I kidding? He *is* funny. She flicks her hair and places her hand on his arm. Flirting 101, How to get a guy to notice you. Well, she's nailed that and mastered it because he's definitely noticing her right now.

His head turns in my direction, and his eyes catch mine. We stare at each other for fifty years, or that's what it seems like. I wish I knew what he was thinking. Is he missing me as much as I'm missing him?

Was it his fault or mine that we're not speaking? I have no idea.

Then it happens.

He turns his attention away from me and back towards Chelsea, but being the horrible person she is, notices that he is looking at me and doesn't like it. The next thing I see is her mouth on his. She puts her hands on either side of his face and kisses him, full-on, in front of everyone.

What. A. Bitch.

I take a step back as though someone has punched me in the stomach. I can't watch anymore but yet I can't stop watching. He doesn't stop the kiss, in fact, he gives full consent to it, even putting his hand on her waist. Bile rises in my throat. I turn and head towards the kitchen. I can't get out of there fast enough. *They kissed.*

I walk through to the kitchen, trying to find Heidi or Anna.

*I will not cry. I will not cry.*

What is happening to me? Why do I have such a problem with this? He can kiss whoever he wants. He isn't mine to own, but god, the adrenaline rushes through my veins as I stop myself from punching her. I want to march over there and tell him he has no right. It's obvious that I have serious issues when it comes to mine and Ed's relationship.

*Deep breaths, calm the hell down, or everyone will notice.*

Everyone is already wondering why we're not talking and spending time together. They're going to put two and two together and get ten.

Heidi walks into the kitchen and sees my face. "What's the matter?"

I shake my head, "Bitchface and Edward kissing in the living room has made me want to throw up."

Her eyes widen, "Wow, really?"

"Yeah, she saw I was there and planted one on him, but he didn't run away, quite the opposite."

She shakes her head. "Aw, Harper. Why don't you just admit it? We *know*."

What is she talking about? "Know what?"

"You and Edward. Something is going on with you two. You have feelings for him. You're jealous."

I shake my head. This is what everyone is thinking. "No, Heid. It's not like that. I just can't handle us not being together all the time. It's always only been him and me. I can't cope that I have to share him."

She shakes her head and sighs. "You will have to admit that you like him eventually."

I'm getting so fed up with people saying that something's going on between us. It's because of them and their comments that things have gotten weird between us.

"Let's change the subject."

She narrows her eyes at me for a moment and then nods. "Fine, but we're friends, yeah? You can trust me."

I nod, "I know, thanks, Heid." I try to lighten the atmosphere. "So, what about you? Do you have your eye on anyone?"

She scrunches her nose. "In this place? No, k not." Heidi is into music in a big way. She isn't into basketball or basketball players. She comes with me for something to do. I've heard her sing, she has the most beautiful voice I've ever heard but says she'll never sing in front of other people, she's too nervous. Anna and I try to talk her into it all the time. She is fantastic, she plays the electric guitar too. She is seriously cool, but no one knows it but us.

My phone pings as I'm getting a drink. I've set it to get notifications on emails for if I get one from *Rookiewithgirls*. The more I think about that name, the more I think he's wrong. Rookie? I don't think so.

*You look so pretty. You by far outshine all the girls in this room by a million to one.*

Wow, he can see me. He's seen me. I message back;

*This is becoming seriously unfair, you can see me, but I can't see you.*

*You can if you look hard enough.*

What does that mean?

*Are you going to introduce yourself?*

*Maybe next time.*

Hmmm… yeah, right.

I get another one. *You're sad tonight.*

Is it that obvious? I need to snap out of it and put on my fake happy persona.

*Sorry, I'll snap out of it.*

*Want to talk?*

*In person?*

*Well, I can call you? I have a voice changer app. It wouldn't be any fun if you heard my real voice now, would it?*

Hmmm, does that mean I've spoken to him before if he thinks I'll recognise him?

Do I want him to call me? Why not? It might take my mind off Edward.

I send him my number. *Sure, call me.*

*Go into the garden. I'll call you when you get out.*

Not sure if it's sweet that he can see me or downright stalkerish. At what point should I be worried? It's a fine line.

I do what he says and step outside, and butterflies start to swirl within me. Am I really going to be talking to him? Hopefully, I'll get him to drop a clue about who he is.

My phone rings in seconds, an unknown number. I answer it.

"Hey." His voice sounds weird because of the voice changer.

"Hey, it's you."

"It's me, Beautiful. Why so sad?"

I sigh. "I'm having friend issues."

"Want to talk about it?"

I shake my head, even though he can't see me... or can he? "Not really, so... you're calling me."

"Yup, I couldn't stand seeing the prettiest girl in the room look so sad."

"I was trying to hide it."

"Yeah, I could tell, but I saw through it."

"Are you a weirdo?"

He chuckles. "I don't think so. Are you?"

"Of course not! But I don't know who you are, do I? What if you're this weird guy?"

There's silence until he says, "No, I get it, I could be a weirdo. I'm not, though - you're going to have to take my word for it. Please trust me."

I could do that, I guess. "Yeah, OK. I can do that. Are you enjoying the party?"

"Ugh, no - I'm hating every minute."

"Do you come to Connor's parties all the time?" I need info on this guy!

"Yeah, but I usually have a good night, although my night got better when I saw you. New dress? It looks good on you—but then, you could make a paper bag look good."

"Ha, I've got to say, this flattery is working. Glad you like it."

"You been shopping?"

I roll my eyes. "Yeah, I'm all about the shopping."

"You sound bored. Am I right in thinking that there's more to Harper than just shopping?"

I stare at my feet, "I guess, but everyone expects you to act a certain way, right?"

There's something about the anonymity that is helping me open up to him.

"No, I don't get that. You should be able to be yourself."

"It's not that easy. I think it's easier for guys."

"Yeah, maybe, but it must be exhausting putting on a front constantly."

Wow, this guy can really see through me. I hope it's not as easy for anyone else.

"Sometimes it gets old, yeah."

I can hear the party in the background and a girl's voice but can't make it out whose it is.

Suddenly he says, "I've got to go. Maybe I can call you again sometime?"

I frown. "Do you have a girlfriend?"

He makes a snorting noise, "There's only one girl I'm interested in. No, I don't have a girlfriend."

I sigh with relief, "OK then, yeah, you can call me again."

We end the call with goodbyes, and I replay the conversation in my mind. No clues about who this guy is. Maybe I should have a wander around, see if anyone catches my eye. My shoulders droop as I turn around and step inside, ready to put on my happy party girl face and - even worse - face Edward with Chelsea.

When I step into the living room, I come face to face with Abraham.

"Hey Harper, want to hang with me for a bit?"

I watch his face for any tell. Is it him? Should I ask him? I should talk to him, see if anything he says matches? I see Edward glance my way out of the corner of his eye. He's standing with his friends now, Chelsea is nowhere to be seen.

I turn to Abraham, "Sure, that might be nice."

He leans into me and puts his hand on my hip, "I'm so glad you're talking to me."

"Well, I guess I don't know you very well, so I should give you a chance."

"You are gorgeous." His eyes run up and down my body, taking in my dress.

I blush, never used to guys telling me that, "Thank you, you want to get a drink?"

He nods, "Sure."

We make our way into the kitchen. No one else is in there. He goes to the big container full of drinks surrounded by ice and hands me a beer. I shake my head, "Coke for me, please."

He shrugs and turns around to get me the can of coke.

He returns and stands close, "I've been nervous to text you after I got your number, and I didn't want to be too pushy."

I shake my head, "It's fine, honestly."

He pulls the ring pull on his can of lager, and, typically for how my night is going, it sprays all over me. Luckily my dress is dark, but my chest and arms and legs are drenched. Great. Just great.

"Oh my god, I'm so sorry, here, let me help."

He grabs the kitchen roll and comes towards me. He isn't going to… yes, he is, he starts to dab my chest. No regard for my personal space.

"Er, Abraham," I grab his hand and pull it away when he's jerked backwards.

His eyes are wide as he falls backwards, and behind him, Edward is standing there, looking murderous.

"What the hell, dude?" Abraham says to him, picking himself up off the floor.

"Did you have your hands on her? Did you have your hands on her, you dickhead?" Edward's hands are in fists and his face is bright red. If it was physically possible, steam would come out of his ears. I've never seen him this way.

Abraham holds his hands up. "I..." He doesn't even get a chance to get his words out before Edward grabs his top and pushes him backwards. Abraham hits the floor again.

"Edward!" I shout.

Others have come rushing into the kitchen to see what the commotion is. Everyone is going to think that Abraham has been doing something he shouldn't, but he wasn't. Yeah, he was in my personal space, but he was only trying to help. I'm sure it was innocent.

I go to Edward and put my hands on his chest - he glares at me. "Ed, it's fine. It's nothing."

He leans in so that his face is an inch away from mine. "He had his hands on you."

"Only because we spilt a drink, he was wiping it. It was nothing."

He stares at me for a moment, his chest moving up and down rapidly as he's trying to process what I've said.

"He shouldn't have done it, I could have done it myself, but it was nothing."

A girl's voice from behind us says, "Hmmm, sounds like someone got jealous to me."

He stiffens at this and steps back from me. "Sorry, I just thought," he shakes his head, "Shit!" And barges out of the room. I glance at Abraham, give him a small smile, and leave the room to clean up in Conor's bathroom.

I check out the damage in the mirror. Well, the beer avoided my hair, at least, but everywhere else is sticky. Guess it's home time for me. What was Edward thinking? I've never seen him act that way. No doubt we'll be the talk of the school on Monday, and *oh god*, Chelsea is definitely going to have something to say.

I make my way home alone. It's not too far, but it still gives me the creeps walking alone in the dark. Even though it's my imagination, I can't help feeling that someone is following me.

## Chapter Nine

♥

Harper

I was right. Monday was a nightmare, there was gossip, but if I'm honest, Edward got the brunt of it more than me. People understood why he acted the way he did. Abraham kept his distance from me—I can't say I blame him.

To cheer me up, *Rookiewithgirls* left me a carnation in my desk in history lesson, with a note;

*Google the meaning.*

I googled it. It symbolises pure love, luck, and affection for the girl in your dreams. It cheered me up so much. I wanted to tell Ed, but we hadn't spoken since the incident on Saturday night. I thought that he'd have tried to find me afterwards but nothing - I didn't hear from him yesterday. Instead, I spent the day in my room, trying not to wallow in self-pity... it didn't work.

And at last, Monday is over, now to pack my school bag for Tuesday. I grab my books when I hear someone coming upstairs.

"Knock knock." Sounds like Edward at my bedroom door, but different. I frown.

"Come in."

It's Cooper, which shocks the hell out of me. It's not often I talk to Cooper these days. We're friends, of course we are - we grew up together, but we don't have much in common, and unlike Edward and me, who got closer and closer, we drifted apart.

Cooper is quiet and keeps himself to himself, like, *a lot*. I don't know what he does or where he goes half the time - I don't even know his friends. He hangs with a couple of guys in sixth form, but I'm not sure how close he is to them.

"Can I talk to you? Your mum let me in." His gaze is intense. It makes me shuffle my feet and glance away. How can they be identical twins and be so different? One puts me at ease, and one makes me so uncomfortable I want to run away.

"Sure you can. What's up?"

"It's about half term next week."

I sigh, like always at half term, I'm supposed to be going to the Beaumont house - the house that Pete and Carrie, Ed and Coop's parents, own. It's been in the family for generations, and since the Locks are like second parents to me, it's my go-to holiday place. When my dad left, and it was only my mum and me, she couldn't afford to take us on holiday, so I went with them. I go with them all the time. I have my own room there, I'm part of the furniture.

"I think I might not go," I mumble.

"I know you and Ed have had a thing. He's bloody miserable at the moment. What happened?"

Where do I start? "It's complicated."

"What's complicated about it? You're either friends, or you're not."

"It's not that simple. There's a girl involved, not to mention that something happened at Connor's party on Saturday."

He nods. "I heard what he did at the party. What's happening with the girl?"

"He doesn't want to spend time with me anymore." I say sadly.

He frowns as though he doesn't understand it, "Ed said that?"

I shrug. "It was his decision."

His eyebrows raise, "Really? Because he tells it differently."

"I doubt Edward's new girlfriend will like me going to the Lakehouse."

"I don't give a shit, and she's not his girlfriend."

"You sure about that?"

"She is sniffing around, but you've been coming to the lake house since you were ten. You're coming, and that's that."

"I don't want to make things awkward for you."

"So don't, sort it out before we go. He's in the den, pining over you. Go and see him."

He turns to leave.

I call out, "Thanks, Coop."

He raises a hand but doesn't look back at me and says, "Can't be doing with this teenage drama." As he runs down the stairs.

But we *are* teenagers...

Think that's the longest conversation I've had with Cooper in three years. Nice to know he still cares. I check my mobile; *Rookiewithgirls* and I are in the middle of a messaging sprint.

I messaged him to thank him for the carnation. It was super thoughtful, and I had an Edward shaped hole I had to fill. So I ask him;

*Should I make up with my best friend?*

*Do you miss him?*

*How do you know it's a him?*

*Everyone knows you and Edward have fallen out. You're inseparable usually, but you*

*haven't spoken to each other all week."*

I hate it when I'm the centre of gossip, but I guess that was inevitable.

*Yeah, Edward and I aren't on the best of terms.*

*Is it because he started seeing Chelsea?*

*No, of course not. Why do you say that?*

*Thought maybe there was a possibility you were jealous.*

*Why does everyone keep saying that? Of course I'm not jealous.*

*Do you not like Chelsea?* Now, there's a loaded question if ever I've heard one. I can't stand her, she's not a nice person *at all*, but everyone sees me with her and being friendly with her all the time. What do I say to that?

*It's nothing to do with Chelsea and more to do with mine and Ed's relationship.*

*Do you have feelings for him?*

My stomach drops as I read those words. Do I have feelings for Edward? I can't stop thinking about him all of a sudden. It's the stupid bus lot crew, putting that idea in my mind again, I was never gonna see him that way again, until then, but they gave me hope. Hope that he may see me that way, and now? Now my head is completely messed up. Why do I have such a problem that he's now decided to show an interest in girls? Am I just jealous because he usually spends all his time with me, and now I'm being dumped or is it more? I miss him. Maybe I can't have any answers to all this until I actually talk to him, sort out this silly argument. Right, that's decided. He's in the den, so that's where I'll go. I don't message him because I already know he's there - no time like the present.

I can't hear anything as I step into the den, and Edward doesn't turn around. He has headphones on and he's staring at his phone, as though he's willing it to ring. I hope he's not waiting to hear from *her*. I tap him on the shoulder.

He startles, spins around, knocks over his drink. "Jesus, Buttercup. What the hell?"

My heart hurts hearing him say my nickname, and I can't help but laugh that I scared him to death.

"Sorry, didn't mean to creep up on you there."

He shakes his head, "Really? 'Cos you did a damn good job of it."

I punch him on the shoulder, "Shut up, you wuss."

He fiddles around wiping the spilt coke and picking the can up, then he turns to me. "I'm glad you've come."

"I figured we need to talk."

"How did you know I was here?"

Should I tell him that Cooper has been fighting his corner? Best not, he might not like it that Cooper has got involved.

I shrug. "I took a chance and got lucky."

He nods, "Are we going to sort this out?"

I swing around and sit down next to him on the blanket, the one only a week earlier we fell asleep together and all was good.

"I want to." I look at him, and those green eyes of his are watching me.

"Good, so do I. I wanted to talk to you, but I didn't want you to be mad. I went about our last conversation all wrong. I'm sorry I upset you. You can't honestly believe that I wouldn't want to hang with you anymore or spend time with you. I mean that when there's a girl in the picture, I can't be with you as much."

I get that I do, I *hate* it, but I get it. "I understand. I overreacted too. I guess I'm used to being the only important person in your life, other than Coop, of course. I mean, yeah, we have other friends, but it's always been us two."

He nods, "I know."

"I guess I'm going to have to get used to the fact that it can't be like that anymore."

"We'll always be friends - it won't be like you're thinking, I'm just trying to keep everyone happy."

"And that's what you want? Are you happy too?"

"I'm trying to find a happy balance, a few of the guys at school have said that it's not healthy how much I hang with you." He must see my face as he holds his hands up. "They said that, not me. They said that *maybe,* it would put off any girl that likes me, trying to start something with me, because they'd be jealous of you."

"Why do your friends even have to comment? I want everyone to leave us alone. I get it though. It goes the same the other way around too, I guess. Maybe you'd put off my future suitors, sir." I put on a posh British accent and flick my hair back, grinning at him.

"They'd be mad if they let me put them off."

He says stuff like this, but I don't know if he means it like I'm taking it. Does he mean that nothing should stop a guy if he likes me because I'm a catch? Or does he mean because it is so totally platonic between us? Argh, I'm sick of trying to guess what's going on in his head.

"If I started to see someone too, we'd hardly see each other at all. I'd hate to grow apart and be strangers. I do love ya, you know. I'm scared of that happening." My voice sounds small and timid. I don't think I've ever told him I loved him before, but I do.

He smiles and gives me the dimples. I love it. When that smile is directed at you, and you know you're the cause of it, just wow. He opens his arms so that I'll lean in for a hug, which I do. His warm, firm body presses up against mine and his arms close around me. His head bends, and he kisses my hair. "I love you too." My stomach flips, and I squeeze a little tighter.

"Promise me we'll always be friends?" I mutter into his t-shirt, fighting against the tears that are trying to battle their way out.

"I promise. Now can we forget all this crap and go back to normal?"

I nod against his chest. "I would love that."

"So, you're still coming to the Lakehouse?"

I nod, "I want to, but won't Chelsea mind?"

"You've been coming on holiday with us since we were little kids. That doesn't change, no matter who I see, yeah?" I don't answer and he's silent for a while as he runs his hand up and down my back, "She has no reason to be jealous, right?"

*Does she?*

## Chapter Ten

♥

Harper

It's here! Half term!

The rest of the week goes fast. Between messaging *Rookiewithgirls*, talking to Abraham, and travelling to school with Edward, things went back to normal. My popularity didn't take too much of a hit at the party. Chelsea seemed quite pleased that I seemed to have something going with Abraham.

Eventually, Abraham came to talk to me. Edward doesn't seem to approve of whatever I've got going there, and he doesn't think he's *Rookiewithgirls* - apparently, he's not thoughtful enough, who knows? We will see.

Abraham asked me if I wanted to go out with him. I said yes, but I told him I was away for half term, so he said he'd text me next week and we'd arrange it for after the school holidays.

I'm terrified. I've never been out with a boy before. What if it goes well and he wants to kiss me? Something that no one knows about me, not even Edward, is that I've never kissed anyone before. I know I'm going to have to go for it and get it over with, but what if I'm rubbish, maybe he would tell everyone, and everyone will laugh at me. I don't want to come across as inexperienced. So yeah, kind of terrified about that date.

Time to go. I hand Pete the suitcase outside of his house. "Wow, what have you got in here?"

I laugh, "Pete, you know I need to prepare for all weathers, and I have to have the shoes to go with it."

"Hmmm, correct me if I'm wrong but don't you practically live in your pyjamas and jogging pants at the Lakehouse."

I gasp, "How dare you!"

"Harper, every time you do this. You say you're going to get dressed up, and then every time you live in the same stuff all week. I don't care what you wear, but why keep taking all this stuff?"

"*Please*? You don't understand. I have to plan for all occasions, and Ed said he'd take me into Bowness for the day, plus we'll be going out for tea—see, that's three outfits and three pairs of shoes right there."

He rolls his eyes, "Fine."

We have the same conversation every time I hand him a suitcase, he always gives in. I love him - he's the dad that I don't have—the dad that my dad should be. I barely have a relationship with my dad now, but Pete and I have a banter like father and daughter should have. I'm so thankful I've got him.

I turn to Mum, who has seen me outside, and give her a hug. "Bye Mum, take care of yourself while I'm gone."

"Oh, I will, I'll be working mostly, and Gary will be around too." Gary is mum's new flavour of the month. I wonder how long he will last.

"OK, I'll text you."

She leans in and kisses me on the cheek, and I climb into the Land Rover. Ed and Cooper have driving lessons, but neither are advanced enough to take their test yet, so we all pile into Pete's car. Luckily, it's big.

Carrie, his mum, glances back at us, all squashed in - I'm in the middle.

"Rose between two thorns there, sweetheart?" she says, grinning at me.

I grin back, "You know it."

Ed nudges me, "Hey, and hey Mum!"

Coop shakes his head and plugs his earphones in.

And we set off, as I wave to Mum until we round a corner.

I watch the many fields and farmhouses pass by the window as we zoom down the cottage lanes to the house. It's hard to believe that only an hour away from where we live is this beautiful countryside. The area where we live is nice, but it's built up, urban with not much greenery, so getting away and coming here, it's my paradise. Surrounded by nature.

I have brought my paperwork and books with me to work on the competition. It has to be completed this week while I'm away so that I can send it off. I'm nearly there and happy with how it is going, but I need to put the finishing touches on it.

I recognise the area as we by-pass the familiar buildings. We're nearly here - my happy place! As we drive down the long driveway, my heart fills with love, happiness and completeness.

My one favourite place on earth. I love the peace - I love that I can one hundred per cent be myself here without the worry of anyone seeing me. It's just me, Ed, Coop and his mum and dad, my mum sometimes comes, but not this time. It's a huge five-bedroomed farmhouse, with has a granny flat annexe. This place is seriously worth a fortune. The last time they had it valued, it was worth over a million.

Sometimes they let it out but only to people they know or from recommendations to people they trust. It's seriously impressive. When Mum comes, we stay in the annexe together, but I will stay in the main house with everyone else while it's only me. There's a bedroom downstairs, which I've claimed as mine, and the boys have their own room upstairs. I used to share with the boys when I was younger, but obviously, as we got older, it wasn't appropriate for us to share, so they put me downstairs in the guest bedroom - everyone calls it Harper's room.

The garden… oh my god, don't get me started on the garden. Pete and Carrie let me loose on it a couple of years ago and let me design the layout, not that it needed much tweaking - sometimes you don't mess with perfection. It is the picture of serenity and beauty. I love spending time sitting in there, taking it all in. Mum laughs at me, she says I'm the next Alan Titmarsh —some old gardener on TV, yes, I do know who he is because I've watched every one of his programmes. What can I say? I'll take my tips and knowledge any way I can get them.

We park and get out of the car. I step outside of the front door and turn to everyone, "Shh… guys, you hear that?"

Everyone goes quiet, and Carrie asks, "What are we listening to exactly?"

"That's just it… nothing… silence, apart from nature working its magic. Best. Place. Ever!"

Edward walks over to me, "We all love this place, Cup, but you love it enough for all of us."

I beam at him. He's right, I do. They all laugh at me and I don't care one little bit.

We unpack our things with plans to meet in the conservatory for dinner. A housekeeper comes to care for the place when no one is here, and Carrie had her come and stock the fridge and freezer with lovely homemade food, ah to be rich, Mum and I, we do OK, we live in a nice big house in a good area, but we don't have much spare cash. Mum works hard to provide for us. Since dad left, she has been under a lot of pressure to cover the bills, thankfully dad didn't leave her in the lurch money-wise, but things are not plain sailing.

Carrie and Pete are seriously loaded. Lucky for me because it means I get to come to this place.

After we have finished the steaming hot and tasty cottage pie followed by a delicious Victoria sponge, I lean back in my chair and clutch my stomach. "I have never eaten so much in all my life."

Cooper eyes me, "Er yeah, you did, last time we were here."

I narrow my eyes at him. "Shut up. Do you have to remember everything?"

I turn to Ed, "You know what I need to do."

Edward and Cooper roll their eyes at each other.

"What?" I ask them.

"You are so predictable. You want to go to the lake."

I do, I really do, we've been here like two hours and I haven't seen it yet.

I nod and grin.

Edward stands. "Come on, I'll take you."

I stand and clap, "Yey! Let me grab my phone."

Ed shakes his head. "You don't always have to have that thing attached to your hand. Leave it here."

"No! I want to take pictures."

He rolls his eyes but says nothing.

Once I've put a jacket on, we head out. It's 8pm, so the sun is setting.

"Ed, it's going to be gorgeous at this time of night."

"Yeah, it's awesome here. Nice to chill, not have anywhere to be, just hang out."

We walk in silence for a little while, I want to ask him about Chelsea, but I also don't want to spoil my mood.

He breaks the silence first. "So, what's happening with Anonymous Emailing Guy?" he glances my way.

"Not much, we message, and he seems nice, but I still don't know who he is, and after I spoke with him at the party, I'm still none the wiser. I still think it might be Abraham, but I could be totally wrong - who knows."

"I honestly don't think it's Abraham."

I shrug, "I don't know. He's been nice lately, not half as bad as I thought he was. Once you get to know him, there's more to him than you think."

"Huh, I don't know about that. Will you go out with him?"

"Who? *Rookiewithgirls* or Abraham?"

He shrugs, "Both."

"Well, *Rookiewithgirls* doesn't seem in any rush for us to meet. In fact, I'm getting a bit worried that it's someone pulling a prank. I hope I'm wrong about that. But Abraham did actually ask me out a couple of days ago."

He stops walking and grabs my arm. "*What?* When?"

"When we get back from here, but I'm terrified."

He frowns. "Are you scared of him?"

"Don't be silly, not like that. I'm just nervous about it."

"Why would you be nervous?"

*Because I've never kissed a guy, that's why.*

I shake my head. It's too embarrassing to say, "It doesn't matter. Anyway, there's *Rookiewithgirls* to consider. If he finds out that I go out on a date with Abraham and it's not him, maybe he'll get upset? But I suppose that's his problem - he's the one who won't tell me who he is."

"Do you like *Rookiewithgirls*?"

"There's nothing to dislike, really. He's sweet, funny and seems to care about me. And he tells me I'm beautiful, like, every day."

We reach the top of the hill to the lake and climb over it. I gasp and grab Edward's arm. The sun is setting behind the trees, and it's as beautiful as I remember.

He clears his throat, "You are, you know."

"What?" I turn to him, distracted by the view. I can't even remember what we are talking about.

"Beautiful." He says seriously.

My head snaps around to him as my breath hitches in my throat. Did Edward just say I was beautiful? Why is my heart beating so fast?

"Thanks, Cap. You've never said anything like that before."

He shrugs, "It's true. Anonymous Guy is probably not approaching you because he knows you are out of his league."

"But he says he's popular."

"I'm not talking about popularity. Look at you, you're gorgeous, you have everything, not only pretty and a fantastic figure, your personality is OK, I guess, too."

I bat him on the arm.

"No, I mean it, you're funny, kind, smart, and so talented. I don't get why you hide that from the rest of the world, but I'm honoured you show that to me."

I regard him for a moment, letting the words sink in. He's never said this stuff to me before. But how can he not get why I keep the gardening stuff a secret? He can't be serious. "That's sweet of you to say all that, but you honestly don't know why I hide the gardening stuff?"

He frowns. "No, I don't. I know you want to be popular, but you should do you and be proud of it - who you are is pretty amazing."

I want to tell him. He still has no idea that I heard him all those years ago tell his friend that he could never like me, but more importantly, *why* he would never like me. He said he would never like me because of who I was - because I was so into gardening, and it was weird. I need to tell him I heard. What would he say to that? It's like he doesn't remember saying those things. Has he changed his mind?

He stares at the lake and speaks, "Can I ask you something?"

"Of course."

"Do you think that if we hadn't grown up together, that we didn't know each other before high school, that we would have been attracted to each other?"

Wow, where the hell did this come from, and what do I say to it? He never knew that I had a crush on him years ago. I made myself switch off from that after hearing what he said. He obviously didn't like me in that way, but if he wants me to be honest about now, then yes, he's gorgeous - hot with the personality to match - but what if it becomes weird between us? But maybe he's having self-confidence issues and needs a little reassurance? How best to play this?

"That's a weird question."

He shrugs but continues to stare at me.

"You know you're hot, right?"

He gives me a lop-sided grin.

I roll my eyes. "Practically all my friends drool over you - don't tell them I told you that, and even though you're so well, hot, you're a good guy... mostly, I mean you have your moments, but, yeah, you're a good guy and truth be told a pretty amazing person. So yeah, maybe if we hadn't known each other before, something could have happened, who knows?"

He shifts, so his body is facing mine, and his hand reaches up and brushes my hair down my back. "Maybe things would have been different if we hadn't been friends from being babies. You're special, but you don't know you're special. Sometimes I feel like it's my job to convince you that you don't need to be popular to be special - one day, I will make you realise."

This is the opposite of what he said years ago. "But what you said?"

"What did I say?"

I shake my head. I don't want to get into it now. "Never mind. I guess we'll never know, will we?"

"We could maybe find out."

"What do you mean?"

He shrugs and fixates on the lake, "I don't know... don't you ever wonder if there's anything there between us, or could be?"

"I... I..." I'm lost for words. I hadn't wondered until lately - since then, it's crossed my mind more than once. It worries me a little that I hate the thought of him with Chelsea.

We never have deep conversations like this, and my mouth has gone dry with the way he's looking at me. So intense, and the light brown flecks in those brown eyes seem to be shining brighter than ever.

His head moves ever so slightly in my direction, and he glances at my mouth.

Wait…

*Is he going to kiss me?*

## Chapter Eleven

♥

Harper

"Ed… Harp… are you here?"

His Mum's voice jolts me back to reality. Edward shakes his head and stiffens. What is he thinking?

The sun setting over the lake is breathtaking - maybe the romantic scenery clouded his judgement for a minute because I seriously thought he was going to kiss me. Wasn't he? I'm pretty sure he was. Things are getting strange. I didn't hate it… the opposite, in fact… but it was strange.

"Yeah, we're over here," I shout, and the tension between us dissipates.

"Ah good, I decided to join you, walk off a bit of that cake."

I smile at her as she links us both, and we walk around the lake for a while. We get chilly after a while and head back.

I unpack and get changed into my pyjamas. We watch TV together. Ed and I haven't been alone since the moment at the lake, and I can't stop thinking about it. We can't talk about what happened or nearly happened. What would I have done if he'd kissed me? I'm seeing him in a whole new light recently. It's like something has shifted between us, but I don't know how to handle it. What would it be like to kiss him? To have his mouth on mine, his hands on me. Butterflies start in my tummy at the thought. Part of me wishes his mum hadn't shown when she did, but part of me is glad that she did. It's exhausting thinking about it all.

When I yawn, Edward glances over, "Someone's bedtime?"

I stand and stretch, "It sure is, night, everyone."

"Night, honey," Carrie says, "we'll keep the noise down. It won't be too long before we go up, anyway."

"Oh, it's OK, you know me, I can sleep through anything."

I glance at Edward, reacalling the night we slept together. He's watching me with a strange expression. I wonder if he's remembering that too.

I walk into my room and flop on the bed. Intense day. I scroll through Instagram - I can't be bothered posting tonight. I'll post pictures of the lake tomorrow. I posted this morning - 575 likes, not too shabby.

There's a post from Chelsea, pouting and posing to perfection, the caption; 'missing my guy' and a sad face.

*Piss off, Chelsea.*

I *do* feel kinda smug. I'm the one here with him - not that it's a competition, but I'm spending the week with him while she pouts about missing him on Instagram. Aw, what a shame Chelsea. Yeah, so what? I can be a bitch sometimes. She deserves it. I'm so tempted to comment, saying something like, 'Aw, he's fine, hun, don't worry, I'm keeping him busy.' but I know my life wouldn't be worth living - it *would* be so much fun, though.

I lie down and start to scroll mindlessly on Snapchat when a message comes through;

Ed; **You still awake?**

Obviously, tonight is on his mind like it's on mine.

Me; **Yeah, what's up?**

Ed; **Nothing.**

Ok Cap, gonna need more than that.

Me; **k.......**

Ed; **We should talk about earlier - when things got weird.**

Hmmm, what do I say to that...

Me; **Yeah, we should. What *was* that?**

The dots appear as though he's replying, then they disappear, then they come back. He's struggling with his reply. I eventually get one back.

Ed, **I'm sorry I made things weird. I've been thinking a lot lately about us, and how we are together, we're good, you know? And I don't know... I guess the guys say to me how hot you are all the time, and it pisses me off.**

Me; **I have no idea what you're trying to say.**

Ed; **I guess that I'm sorry, I didn't mean to say those things out loud, I wasn't thinking.**

Me; **Don't worry, let's forget it, yeah?**

It's a while before he messages me back. Evenutally, I get;

Ed; **Yeah, sure. Night Buttercup.** And a smiley face.

I sigh and put my phone down. I'm glad he's cleared the air—or tried to – the air seems thicker than ever. I re-read the messages—he's been thinking about us a lot? What has he been thinking?

I toss and turn for a while, everything going around in my head, and when I do eventually fall asleep, yup, my dreams are of him.

※※※※※※

The plan when we wake is to go to the spring fayre in Keswick village. We go every year. They make the whole centre of Keswick pedestrianised, there is bunting everywhere, and they have little village stalls dotted around. The stalls can be anything; homemade jams, cakes, crafts, pictures - it's lovely. Every time we go, it seems to be sunny and today is no exception, blue skies all around.

Once I'm up and showered, I pick one of my outfits. I decide on some dark blue cropped jeggings and a blue checked fitted off the shoulder gipsy top. It has a cottagey villagey vibe, I'm sure. I pile my blonde hair on top of my head in a messy bun—I perfected the technique years ago. I put on minimal makeup, I'm on my holidays after all, just some tinted moisturiser and mascara. Not a false lash in sight. I glance in the mirror. I look younger, way younger, but this is me… the me without all the armour.

I can hear voices, which will be Pete and Carrie - unless they are lucky and have got Edward out of bed early. Cooper will stay in his room until the last minute, that's if he even comes at all.

I walk into the kitchen. "Good morning, everyone. Gorgeous day."

Ed spins around, his eyes go down my body as he takes in what I'm wearing, then he gives me one of his grins and winks at me while shoving a croissant in his mouth. "Sure is, Buttercup. You up for a shopping day?"

I try to ignore the fact that every skin cell that belongs to me is tingling because of the wink.

*Stop it, Harper.*

I shake it off. "Aren't I always? Although this one is all food, that works too." It's the most delicious homemade food you would ever taste.

He looks good. He's dressed in dark skinny jeans and a fitted Jack Jones t-shirt, his hair is still a little wet from the shower, and because it's longish, it curls at the ends. He is gorgeous. I have to tilt my head to look up at him. A couple of years ago, he seemed to have a massive growth spurt, and now he towers over me, and his shoulders seem so broad - I don't even know when that happened. But yeah, he is a gorgeous guy, no doubt about it.

The house is in walking distance of the market. It's around twenty-five minutes away by foot. We know when we're getting close because we can hear all the hustle-bustle and can smell all the gorgeous aromas coming from the homemade food stalls.

"You know where I wanna go first?"

I roll my eyes, "Of course - we all know - you want to go to the pie stall."

He nods, his eyes shining, "You know you want a piece of that gorgeous apple pie, all hot, with the ice cream melting. Oh my god, my mouth is watering."

I can't fight the grin. He's like a little kid again when we come here. After the pie, he will want to go to the fudge stall, without a doubt the best fudge I have *ever* tasted, then his crazy sugar high will follow.

There are a couple of rides in the centre, and they have put on a land train, it's the prettiest place on earth.

Cooper sighs, "I guess it's apple pie then, you know… at ten am in the morning."

"Time doesn't matter here, brother, you know that. I guess, seeing as your acting as though it's not a big deal and I'm dragging you there, that you won't want any?"

Cooper smirks. "I didn't say that."

Edward nods, "Yeah, thought so."

"What about you, Buttercup?" he says, coming close and draping his arm around my shoulders, making butterflies come awake in my tummy.

"Bring on the pie." I croak.

We're soon stuffed, sat on a grass verge, watching everyone pass by. Pete and Carrie are still browsing, and Cooper is sitting with Ed and me.

Ed leans into me. "Before I buy and eat anything else, shall we walk up the hill?"

I groan. "Oh god, that sounds way too energetic. The views are something, though. It *would* walk off my apple pie, and fudge, and cookies, oh dear… yeah I'd better do it."

He jumps up and looks at Cooper. "You comin' bro?"

Cooper shakes his head and smirks. "You're being all energetic now because you're on a sugar high, but what happens when you crash?"

Ed shrugs. "Well, hopefully it will be at the top of the hill, and we can have a snooze in the sun."

That does sound like bliss. I hold my hand out so that he'll pull me up. "Come on, let's do it.

We tell Cooper to tell his mum and dad that we'll see them back at the house. We go to a nearby stall for a bottle of water each and make our way to the entrance path for the climb.

We're around halfway up, and I'm getting out of breath when I get a text. It's Abraham with a text asking what I'm doing today. My heart doesn't leap when I see he's contacted me, which it should, at least a little.

"Time out, Cap, I need a sit-down." I gasp.

"You are so unfit. Maybe you should try going for a run sometime."

I scrunch up my face, "Now why the hell would I do that?

He points at my phone. "Who was that?" He tries to peer over my shoulder, so I hold my phone close to my chest so that he can't see the screen.

"It's Abraham, seeing how I am."

He shakes his head as he sits on the ground next to me. "I still can't believe you're giving him the time of day."

"Yeah… well, I feel the same about you and Chelsea."

"Chelsea and I, it's not, it doesn't… oh doesn't matter."

"No go on." I need to know what's going in his head about Chelsea.

He shrugs, "It means nothing really. We're just having fun."

"But you kissed her," I whisper.

He shakes his head, "I'm sorry you saw that. I didn't mean to…"

"You didn't mean to kiss her?" Doesn't he realise how ridiculous that sounds?

"No, it kind of ... well, she went in for the kiss... I guess I didn't pull away. I didn't want to cause a scene at the party."

"Is that the only time you've kissed her?"

He nods. "Yeah, just that time. What about you and Abraham? Have you guys kissed?"

My eyes widen. Is he kidding? "No way!"

"Why do you say it like that?"

I blush. I can't help it, the heat rises in my cheeks.

"Harp, what's up?"

"I'm stressed about the whole Abraham thing." I sigh.

"Why? He's not being an arse with you, is he?"

I shake my head, "No, nothing like that. It's just..." *Oh god, can I say this out loud*? "Fine. Don't tell anyone, OK?"

He makes a cross shape on his chest. "Cross my heart."

"I've never... I don't know how to... I don't have any experience with guys."

"What do you mean? You've kissed a guy before."

I shake my head and glance up at him through my lashes, barely able to return his gaze. "No, Ed, I haven't."

"*What*? You get tonnes of attention from guys?"

"Well, yeah, I guess, but I've never even been out with a guy."

"Of course you have," He stares into the distance as though trying to remember, "Wait, you've never even been on a date?"

"No, it's so embarrassing - everyone assumes - but no, I have no idea what I'm doing."

"Jesus, I didn't know."

I shrug, "Well, now you know."

We're silent for a time while he processes what I've told him and while I die of embarrassment.

"It comes naturally, you know, you don't have to think about it. When you're kissing someone you like, you have to go with the flow, and it all goes well."

"I'm scared that if I kiss Abraham, and it's not good, or he can tell I don't have any experience, that he'll tell everyone, and I'll be a laughingstock."

He's silent for so long that I start to wonder if he's zoned out.
"Edward?"

He shakes his head and stands up, holding his hands out so that he can pull me up. When he does, we are standing close together, facing each other.

He dips his head down to say to me quietly. "I could help you."

"How?"

"You can practice on me."

My eyes widen. He can't be serious, "Get lost, Cap."

"I'm serious. Think about it, you can practice on me, and if you like, I can even give you marks out of ten." He waggles his eyebrows.

I roll my eyes, "Gee, that sounds soooo tempting."

He shrugs, "It's the perfect solution. You wouldn't be inexperienced because you'd have kissed me so you wouldn't be as stressed when the time came."

Hmmm, does he have a point?

"Think about it. Come on."

We make our way up the rest of the hill. We walk in silence because all I can think about is his suggestion. I could practice on him, and no one would ever know.

Should I go for it?

## Chapter Twelve

♥

Harper

We're nearly at the top, just one more ridge and we're there, not without a lot of complaining from me. Why do all the nicest views have to be at the top of something?

Edward says it's that way so that you appreciate it all the more. I'm not so sure - I'd appreciate it even more if I didn't have to climb anything.

Did Edward really say I could kiss him? It's a crazy suggestion but one I'm so tempted to go with. It would solve the issue of being terrified to kiss anyone. Everyone presumes I have experience with guys now, so I can't exactly turn around and tell everyone I don't know what I'm doing. If I kissed Ed, he could tell me if it was rubbish - he's kissed girls before, and he would be able to give me tips.

I shiver at the thought of kissing Ed. What would that be like? To have his mouth on mine, his arms around me. I want that. I don't want things to be weird, but kiss Ed? Jesus, it's not exactly a hardship. He is hot - any girl would jump at it, not that I'd tell anyone, but yeah, if I'm going to learn with someone, he would be a top choice for a teacher.

He turns back to me because I'm trailing behind, "Come on, slowcoach, we're there."

He holds his hand out and I grab it, trying to keep my composure. We step up and are met with the most amazing views. They're out of this world, something that an Instagram picture would not do justice to. It is beautiful.

I turn to Ed, noticing that he still has hold of my hand. "It's gorgeous."

He looks at me and then turns to admire the view, "Breath taking."

A couple of people are milling around - a man with his dog and a couple wearing hiking boots that are making their way back down.

I take a swig of my bottle of water and hand it to Edward, who takes it off me and has a swig. We're sharing a bottle of water, that's almost kissing anyway…

We're silent for a minute, soaking in the rolling hills. If ever there was an opportunity, it's here.

"Ed?"

"Yeah?"

"What happens on the hill stays on the hill, right?"

He frowns at me, "What are you talking about?"

"Let's do it… if it's OK with you." My mouth is dry. I take another drink.

He stares at me blankly. Oh god, he's going to make me say it. I clear my throat. "The practice kiss."

His eyes widen, and he swallows. "Oh, that. Are you sure?"

I shrug, "It's embarrassing, but yeah, it it won't gross you out too much."

"It won't gross me out at all."

I smile at him and give a slight nod. Go time.

"OK, so, we need to be facing each other, like this." He grabs my shoulders, facing me to him. "OK, he will probably, you know, if he's any good," he smirks, "put his hands on your face or your neck like this.

He places his hands on my neck, and goosebumps rise all over my body. This is it, my first kiss - even if it isn't real, it will still be a proper kiss. Ed will always be my first kiss.

"What shall I do with my hands?" I ask him. My voice is hoarse.

He shakes his head a little and fixates on my eyes, "You don't need to do anything unless it feels right, and you want to do it. I'm guessing, if he's into you and wants to kiss you, he will glance down at your mouth while you're talking or while you're close like this."

My heart is going to beat right out of my chest and tumble down the hill.

"Relax, Harper, no one is around, just me and you. You can't mess this up - but even if you somehow did, there's no one here to see."

"Can you feel my heart pounding?" I whisper.

He shakes his head and gives me a small smile as his head bends towards mine.

Just as his mouth is nearly on mine, I mutter, "What if I'm bad?"

He dips in closer, so his face is close to mine. "You won't be."

I glance at his mouth and back to his eyes. Those long eyelashes of his framed his brown eyes perfectly.

I close my eyes as his soft lips land on mine. Electricity runs through my body, so intense that it shocks the hell out of me. Wow, I did not know that was going to happen.

His hand rests behind my neck, and he inhales as he moves his mouth against mine. I relax and move my mouth against his, loving the sensation, his lips are so firm and soft... oh yeah, I like this kissing thing a lot! His hands slide down my arms circle my waist. I take this as my queue to slide my hands around his neck. I finger the hair there, so long that it needs a cut but so so soft.

Is this actually happening? Edward and I kissing.

I part my lips, and Ed takes it as an open invitation to deepen the kiss. I hear the birds above me calling to each other and wonder if this is the most perfect moment of my life. He tastes of apple pie and ice cream... perfect.

We kiss and kiss until, eventually, he breaks off. Our eyes meet, our breathing heavy. Finally, he licks his lips and smiles, "How was that?" our faces are still so close that I could easily close the distance again if I wanted.

"I should ask you that," I whisper.

"Safe to say, Buttercup, you have nothing to worry about."

I grin as though I've just won a kissing award. "No?"

"Hell no." He says and takes a step back, the moment broken between us. Is it wrong that I want to do that again, right now? Who knew kissing felt like that?

"That was... that was great. I never knew kissing was so good or that I waited so long."

He chuckled, "Glad to be of service."

I carried on rambling, "And you know, I never knew it would feel like that, the butterflies and the goosebumps, all that stuff, I thought yeah, mouths touch, move around a little, but that was... that felt... wow." I breathed.

Our eyes lock as his mouth curves in the softest of smiles.

I tilt my head to one side. "What?"

"It doesn't exactly always feel that good, but glad to know you felt it too,"

"Thanks, Ed, that was sweet of you to offer to do that."

He nods, "Yeah, it was so disgusting. You owe me one, big time." He winks at me, and my stomach does the flippy thing again. What is happening to me?

"Haha, shut up. OK, so good at kissing, check, now I've got to know date etiquette, and then I'll be raring to go."

He laughs but stops abruptly. "Wait, I've got an idea!"

"No, Edward, I will *not* kiss you again." I'm relieved that things didn't seem weird between us after that. It felt intense, and at least we were joking around.

"Oh damn. No, I was going to ask, while we're here, I could take you on a pretend date. I'd pick you up and everything, and we can go into Keswick and have a coffee or lunch - like you would do if you were at home."

That's a good idea. "You'd do that?"

He shrugs, "Sure, it's not gonna be that different from us hanging out, anyway, but I'll do date stuff as well. It'll relax you for the real thing."

"Yeah OK, let's do it! When?"

"Tonight? I'll take you into Keswick and well get dinner. But you have to promise me one thing."

"Yeah, what?"

"Promise me that you won't fall in love with me."

I step close to him to punch him on the arm. "Oh, I'll try my very best."

He throws his head back and laughs.

As I watch him, I realise that I'm going to have to try hard not to.

Now, what to wear for my fake date?

## Chapter Thirteen

♥

Edward

We lounge around on the hill for a while. Harper takes lots of pictures to upload to Instagram and a couple of selfies of us both that she said she won't post because of Chelsea. Great.

I can't think straight. That was by far the most fantastic thing I've ever experienced in my life. Better than basketball, better than McDonald's, seriously amazing. And she felt it too, I *know* she did. Only problem is, she believes all kisses are like that. They're not. Nowhere near that level, it was intense, and I felt it in every part of my body.

I didn't want it to end. That's why I came up with the crazy idea of taking her on a date. I'm spending the evening with her as though we're going out, I'm kinda excited. Hell, I'm totally excited. I get to get a glimpse of what it would be like to go out with her, for us to be a couple.

As we make our way down the hill, I grab her hand now and again to help her. It's a companionable silence. We're both lost in our thoughts. I wish I knew what was going on in her head.

"So, where are you taking me tonight?" she asks out of the blue.

"You'll see. I can't tell you now - I want you to have the whole date experience."

She smiles but doesn't say anything. Yeah, tonight is going to be good.

I get home and decide I need a shower after all that trekking. Luckily we have two bathrooms, a small one downstairs and a larger one upstairs, plus mine and Coop's room has an en-suite. When I walk in, Cooper is lying on his bed, eyes closed, earphones in. He's dressed all in black, no surprise there, and he has his legs crossed at his ankles, totally zoned out - he has no idea I'm there. As I walk past, I knock his foot and he looks up and pulls his earphones out.

"You're back, finally."

I nod, "Yeah, for a couple of hours, then out again."

"Where?"

"Harp and I are going for tapas." I'd already decided to take her to a tapas place in Keswick that is good. I have a healthy bank account for a change because of unspent birthday money and my allowance.

"Oh right, I might come. I love the food at that place."

Crap, how do I tell him he can't come? I'm gonna have to come clean.

"Actually, it's only me and Harp tonight."

He raises his eyebrows, "You finally asked her out?"

I'm taken aback, "What?"

"Come on, you think I'm dumb?"

I stare at him blankly.

"Dude, it's obvious - you have a thing for Harper."

"I... I... no I don't."

"You actually trying to lie to me, dude?"

I fixate on my feet. "It's not like that."

"So, you *don't* have feelings for Harp?"

I sigh and run my hands through my hair. "How long have you known?"

"Since before you did."

I wince. "Am I that obvious about it?"

He shrugs, "Maybe, don't know. I notice things about you that others don't, twin thing, you'd have to ask someone else that."

"Do you think Harper knows?"

He snorts, "She hasn't got a clue."

I relax my shoulders. "Thank god."

"So, if you're not taking her out tonight, why can't I come?"

I sit on my bed, tell him about the kiss and the fake date, and swear him to secrecy.

After I'm done, he grins and shakes his head, "I hope you know what you're doing."

"Why, what harm can it do?"

"You're helping her be better with other guys. How can you think that's a good idea? I mean, look at her - she's gorgeous. About the only thing you have going in your favour at the moment is that she's inexperienced when she comes to guys—that's why she lacks confidence in that department—if you give her confidence, the sky is her limit."

"Nah, be fine, just a bit of fun. Besides, I'm gonna be the perfect date, might get her to notice me, you never know."

He shakes his head as I make my way into the shower.

---

I told her to be ready for seven. I decide on skinny black jeans and a grey fitted shirt, figured I should go all out. My navy converse finish the outfit, and I make my way outside. Mum and Dad have gone out somewhere for tea, so it's only the three of us in. I order a taxi on the Uber app, and it says ten minutes away, so I knock on the front door.

No answer.

I knock again. Still no answer. Where is she?

I dial her number, and she answers straight away.

"Hey, where are you?"

"In my room, why?"

"I'm at the front door, ready to collect you for our date, but you're not answering the door."

She gasps, "You nutter! Is that you? I'm ready - I'll come out." She hangs up, and I grin to myself.

She swings open the front door grinning. "What are you like?"

I turn on my date brain, "Hey Harper, I'm here to pick you up for our date."

I check out what she's wearing and immediately regret it. She's so gorgeous. She has a sleeveless fitted white short dress on, at the waist, it flares out into a floaty type of skirt, in a light tan colour, it's short, did I mention that? Did I also mention that she has fantastic legs?

Her eyes run the length of me, "Wow, you're dressed up. Good job I did."

"Of course, it's a date, right?"

She steps out and closes the door.

I lean down and kiss her cheek, breathing in her perfume, a mix of fruity and sultry, with a hint of Harper thrown in, *perfect*.

"Uber will be here in," I check the app, "any minute now."

As I say that, the car pulls onto the driveway. When it pulls up, I open the door for her to climb in, and she looks up at me through those long lashes of hers and smiles. I'm in big trouble here.

Once we're inside, I turn to her. "OK, so this is the rule for tonight, you have to pretend I'm not Edward. I'm some guy that you like that's asked you out. Not me."

She nods, "I can do that. I'm kinda excited."

"Would you say that to a date?" I raise my eyebrows.

"No, sorry, sorry, right, that's it, I'm in character now."

I smile at her, "For the record, be yourself, and you'll do fine."

She blushes under her make-up. I love that I've made her blush. Hmmm, gotta get her to do that again.

The Uber pulls up in front of the tapas, and her eyes shine when she sees it.

She turns to me, "Tapas!"

"Yeah, I chose this place. I've been before, and it's always nice. Do you like tapas?"

She giggles because she's been here so many times with my family and me. "Yeah, I love it. How did you guess?"

I shrug, "Who doesn't like tapas?"

We walk inside, and the server takes us to our table and gives us a menu. We order a couple of cokes and decide on what we're having.

"Tonight's on me."

Her eyes widen, "Oh no way, we can go halves."

I shake my head, "I pay on a date, and that's that."

Her eyes go soft, "Yeah, but..."

"Ah-ah, don't say it."

She giggles and puts the menu down, scanning the room, "It's busy tonight. You were lucky to get a table."

"Yeah, I thought that, at last notice. So, Harper, what made you say yes to the date today." I wink at her to make sure she knows I'm being 'date guy' and not Ed.

"I don't know. I saw you around, and you're always friendly to me and not bad to look at."

"So you find me attractive?"

She shifts in her seat uncomfortably. "Of course, I wouldn't have said yes to the date otherwise - there has to be an attraction, right?"

I nod, "Yes, there does. You look beautiful tonight. You always do, but tonight especially. Maybe because I've wanted to get you on your own for a while now and finally, I have." This is way closer to the truth than I should get.

"Thanks, Cap, I mean, Edward. You look great too."

"It's nice to chat, get to know you better. So, I've seen you around at school, and I know you like to go to Connor's parties. What else do you like to do in your free time."

She pinches her lips together and tilts her head to the side. "I, um, spend a lot of time with friends - my best friend, Ed, mostly we hang out a lot, watch movies, we do everything together."

"So, your best friend is a guy? Isnt that weird?"

She shakes her head, "No, not really. Why?"

I shrug, "Dunno, it's unusual."

She shrugs, "Well, my Ed is the best." Shit, why does it affect me so much that she said 'my Ed'? *Because you want to be her Ed*. It sounds so good.

"Good, I'm glad you have that friendship with someone. Friends are so important. Has it never been anything more between you?"

She shakes her head and stares at her hands. "Actually, I had a little crush on him before high school, but that soon got quelled."

I'm taken aback. She's never said that before, first I've heard of it. "Yeah, what happened?"

"Doesn't matter, that was it. It soon went."

Oh, I need to know what happened there. I mean, it probably wouldn't have gone anywhere. She was a kid with a crush, but what ended it? I don't want to stress her out, so I move on.

"Well, I'm glad it did, or I wouldn't be sitting here with you now, would I?"

"I guess."

The food comes and we tuck in. This part isn't like a date much, as I know exactly what she likes and hand it to her, and she tucks in, "So, usually this part might get a little awkward, I haven't been on that many dates, but the eating part, yeah, I usually like to go for ice-cream, or milkshake or something, so that you're not under pressure.

She nods with her mouthful, "Yeah, I totally wouldn't be scoffing like this if you were a date."

I chuckle, "You'd be nibbling like a chipmunk."

"This date thing isn't so bad when you go with your bestie.

"This time next week, this might be you and Abraham." I try to keep my voice as light as possible, but truthfully, I want to upturn the table at the thought of that.

She shrugs, "You really don't think that he's *Rookiewithgirls*, do you?"

I shake my head. Of course, I know he's not. "No, I don't. Abraham isn't good enough for you."

"You don't know him that well."

"I know enough to know that he's not good enough for you."

Her eyes go wide, and I sigh and run my hands through my hair, "You really have no idea, do you?"

Her eyes widen, "Idea of what?"

"Your worth. You are worth ten of all those girls at school, but you don't think you are."

She tilts her head and narrows her eyes at me. "Is that why you're giving all your time to Chelsea?"

I shake my head, "Chelsea doesn't matter, she's ... oh doesn't matter. Do you want desert?"

I'm so close to telling her the truth right now. At what point do I just sack it and go for it?

## Chapter Fourteen

♥

Harper

Edward is sinking into a grim mood but I'm not sure why. What did I say?

"Hey, shall we go for a walk when we've finished?"

He nods, "Sure, don't try to take advantage of me, though, will you?"

Phew, I have Ed back. "Yeah, you wish."

Although the more I think about that kiss on the hill, the more I believe it was perfect and that I want to do it again, could I get away with saying I wanted extra practice? Hmmm...

Ed settles the bill and we walk outside. It's a warm night, but he hands me his jumper which doesn't go with my dress, but I'm chilly, so I don't care. Keswick is pretty - all the old pubs with their little twinkling lights inviting you in to the cosyness and the small privately owned restaurants that are bursting at the seams with tourists, the main street is quite busy for nighttime.

We veer off down a narrow street and walk along. He grabs my hand as we walk. Startled at the sensation of my hand in his, I glance up at him. "We're on a date, remember?"

I smile. This is nice. So, this is what a date is like.

"How am I doing? Give me marks out of ten."

He drums his fingers on his chin, "Hmmm, a solid two and a half."

I bash him on the shoulder, "Charming! Well, you are a one and a quarter."

He places his hands on his heart, "Ah, you know how to hurt a guy."

"I'm higher than that though, right?"

He looks down at me with an expression on his face I can't decipher, "Maybe a little."

We go quiet for a while, walking along. "What about the kiss?"

"What about it?"

"How many did I score out of ten?"

"Um, a three?"

I know he's joking, but this is a perfect opportunity to do it again. I liked it!

"I can do better than a three, you know, if you give me another shot?"

He clears his throat. "*What*?"

"Let me try again."

I pull his hand that is holding mine so that we come to a stop. He turns to face me.

"I can't kiss you again." His face is serious.

"Why not?"

He shakes his head, pain in his eyes, "I just can't."

Oh my god, I was horrible. "Was I that bad?" I whisper.

He shakes his head, "No, it's not that, not at all, quite the opposite. I enjoyed it too much."

"Well, what's wrong with doing it again?"

"Don't, Harp. Please leave it."

He drops my hand and turns to walk away. What was that about?

I catch up to him and tug on his t-shirt. "Hey, you OK?"

He nods and sighs, "Yeah, we heading back now?"

My stomach dips at the rejection. I asked Ed to kiss me, and he said no. How humiliating.

I nod but say nothing, and we get in the cab back to the house. Great… things are awkward between us now.

I say a quick goodnight and go straight to my room when I get in, wishing I could take back the last hour of my life.

## Chapter Fifteen

Edward

A week later...

I watch Chelsea as she crosses the school courtyard and makes her way over to Harper, who is standing with Heidi and Sam. She hasn't seen me.

She completely ignores Sam and Heidi and makes a point of talking to Harper. Harper does the usual - I watch her do it, no one else would see it, but I do. She switches the charm on like a light switch. This is fake Harper, the one I don't like.

Why can't she just be herself? I don't get it. She has real confidence issues, but why is she always fine with me? She is herself around me one hundred percent, or at least she was until lately. Things have been awkward since I turned down the chance to kiss her again. Why did I do that again? I'm not even sure - I must have been mad. I didn't want to confuse things even more—needed to get my head in the right place. Literally, all I could think of since that first kiss was every single detail of it. The way she felt, how soft her lips were, the sweet scent of her. I couldn't get enough. That's why I said no - my heart can only take so much. She's more and more convinced that the admirer is bloody Abraham. I need to nip that in the bud, but how? I can't come clean yet. If I tell her who it is right now, she will fall out with me altogether. I haven't accomplished my goal at all of making her believe she's worth something.

I want to tell her so badly that I can't stand Chelsea and that *I'm* her mystery guy.

Jasper materialises beside me. "Aw, look at you, watching your two favourite girls."

I nudge his shoulder with mine, "Get lost. It's you who got me into this stupid crazy situation in the first place."

He raises his eyebrows. "Oh, is it now? Because I could have sworn that you came to me whining that you can't carry on as just friends anymore, that you need to know, blah blah blah. Let's not pretend that this is all down to me."

I sigh, "I guess... sorry dude, yeah, it's all me, but I'm completely messing it all up."

"Is any of it working?" he asks.

I shrug, "I don't know, I think I'm making her see me a little differently, but instead of her thinking I'm amazing, its going the other way. Dude, I kissed her, and when she wanted to kiss me again, I said no."

His eyes widen, "Chelsea or Harper?"

I glare at him, "Harper, of course."

"Wow, and..."

"And, it was bloody amazing, everything I thought it would be, but I shouldn't have done it, she's not ready, she doesn't know I've been having these feelings for her, she believes all kisses are like that, but Jesus, Jasper, it was so nice, so right, it felt... I don't know... I love her."

He nods but says nothing.

"So, what's next?"

"Are you ready to tell her you are 'Anonymous Guy' yet?"

I shake my head, "No, not yet. Look at her, she's trying her best to be the most popular girl in year eleven and she's succeeding. 'Anonymous Guy' should be convincing her to be herself, follow her dreams or whatever, but instead she's going the other way."

"Could it be that it's not 'Anonymous Guy' that's sending her the wrong way, but you?"

"Maybe—we're one and the same. Should I come clean and tell her everything and tell her how I feel?"

He shrugs, "You should definitely think about it, but don't jump in with both feet. You said yourself you took her too much by surprise. You should step up the PDA's with Chelsea in front of her. In fact, they're together right now. Let's go over, step it up, and I will watch Harper for a reaction."

"I don't know,"

"You got any other ideas?"

"Fine, come on, not sure I should take relationship advice from a guy that can't even talk to girls but come on."

"Thanks for the vote of confidence. Remind me to return the favour sometime."

We both walk over to the four of them, and they all turn to us. OK, time to act it up. I don't look at Harper, which kills me, instead, I fixate on Chelsea and give her my best smile. She is so happy to have my attention and walks over to me. I slip my arm around her waist and pull her into me, bending down to speak into her ear. "Hey, how you doing?"

She grins at me as though all her birthdays come at once. I can't blame her, she must think I'm so hot and cold. One minute I'm acting as though I like her, and the next minute it's as though I can't stand talking to her.

"Hey, Eddie."

*Ugh, I hate that, don't call me that.* I clamp my mouth shut, and I try my hardest not to look at Harp. She knows I hate being called that.

"Hey gorgeous, you gonna come to the game tonight?" Harper's eyes are burning into me, but she doesn't speak, and Sam and Heidi are watching what's going on.

Chelsea turns her body into mine and places her hand on my chest, gazing up at me. "I'd love to. Want to go to Scoopy Smile afterwards? Isn't that where you and the team usually go?"

Scoopy Smile is an Ice Cream Parlour we hang at sometimes after the games.

I nod, "Yeah, sounds good." OK, that's enough, I can't stand it anymore. I bend to give her a peck on the cheek and quickly glance at the others, making sure that I don't catch Harper's eye because I know the look on her face will kill me.

"Later," I say and walk away, with Jasper following.

When we're out of earshot, he leans into me. "Mission accomplished. She looked suitably crushed."

It split my heart and emotions into two. On the one hand, I can't help but be happy that she seemed bothered. On the other hand, I feel like the biggest arsehole in the world that I'm doing it to her.

"It's because she always goes to my games. I always tell her I want her there, that she's my good luck charm. She will be gutted that I've replaced her."

"Hmmm, I'm not so sure. She seemed gutted before you even brought it up. I'm telling you, there's something there."

*Please let him be right and all this is for something.*

---

Whether that was the right move, too late to change things. The week went by, and Harper and I got more and more distant as she became more and more engrossed in her popular crew. She seemed to switch off from me altogether, and whenever I glanced her way, she was with one of them or taking a selfie or something equally shallow.

I'm losing her. I *miss* her. Like I would miss a limb.

Chelsea was over the moon with the attention she was getting from me, but everything came to a head on Friday.

I scan the lunch cafeteria and see if I can see Harper, but no sign, so I message her through *Rookiewithgirls*.

*Hey beautiful, what are you doing?*

*Hey you, I'm putting the finishing touches on something that I'm applying for to send it off.*

*Oh yeah? What is it?*

*You'll laugh.*

Wait, could she be actually opening up?

*I won't, I promise.*

*OK, so it's a garden landscaping competition. Do you remember I said I was interested in gardening? Well, I love designing gardens and deciding how to place the plants, where everything goes—landscaping, I guess. Anyway I saw this competition, it's so good, and the prize is massive, so I thought I'd give it a go.*

*That is amazing Harper. It's brilliant that you're doing something that you love. Why are you so embarrassed about it?*

*It's not very cool, is it?*

*Why the hell not? Why can you not just be who you want to be and not care whether or not it's cool?*

*I want to fit in.*

This guts me. When will she learn that she is amazing in her own right and she doesn't need to worry about fitting in?

*Trust me, you would fit in just by being you.*

*That's it though, I wouldn't.*

*What makes you so sure?*

*You know that I'm best friends with Ed, right?*

Oh god, where is this going?

*Yeah?*

*OK, so I heard him a few years back talking about me with a friend. He didn't know I was there.*

My stomach plummets to my feet. What was I saying? What did she think she heard about herself? Is this what made her move on from her crush?

*What did you hear?*

I'm terrified of the reply that I'm going to get back.

*He said that he would never be interested in a girl like me - someone who's always a mess with dirt under her fingernails. He said that would never be the kind of girl that guys would go for or that would fit in. Guess it's stuck with me.*

I drop my phone onto the table and put my head in my hands. I groan. I did say that. I remember we were around eleven - I didn't think about Harper that way back then. We were little kids, for god's sake. Shit, she heard that and interpreted it as she can never be herself or she won't be popular. All this is my fault, the way she is, the way she's always striving to be popular, it's all my fault.

Nausea washes over me. I can't deal with this. How has she never said anything to me? I *have* to fix this.

I realise that she's going to be waiting for a response. I can't give her one at the moment, I need to process.

*Gtg, someone needs me, will message asap.*

I put my phone back down and take a deep breath. Calm down, Ed, and figure out the best way to fix this. I've hurt the most important person in my life. God, why didn't she tell me?

I need to fix this, but how?

## Chapter Sixteen

♥

Harper

Was that the right thing to do? I've never told anyone that before. He stopped messaging abruptly, so maybe he agrees with Ed and doesn't know how to reply. I find it so easy to open up to him because I don't see him in person—he's a name on my phone or computer, it's like he's not real - my very own therapy session. I need to remember that he is real and he goes to my school. I may have just told someone something that about myself that I didn't want everyone to know. Someone I maybe can't trust. Damn, I shouldn't have said all that.

I pack everything away, my final drawing is nearly done, and I'm pleased with how it's turned out. I'm in with a chance. I have no idea how many people will enter or how widespread the competition is. The address is local - it's a huge estate. I know of it but never visited. I'm guessing they've advertised Nationwide. All I can do is try.

The knots in my stomach don't dissipate as I rush out of the empty classroom to make my way to the next lesson. My head is down, and I collide with something.

"Argh." My head hit's someone's chest, and everything I'm holding tumbles to the floor.

"Harper." It's Edward. He bends down and grabs all my things and hands them to me. We've hardly spoken all week. He seems sad. Although every time I've seen him at school, he's looked pretty damned happy talking to Chelsea and flirting all over her.

"Sorry I didn't see you."

"Harper, I need to talk to you. It's important."

"Are you OK?"

He shakes his head, "No. I just found out something awful."

"Oh no, what?"

He shakes his head, "I don't want to get into it now. I do want to talk to you, though. I'm out with Chelsea tonight," I try not to show any reaction at that. "But can I see you tomorrow?"

I nod, "Sure."

He seems serious, so I'll need to put my feelings to one side. If he's upset and he needs me - I'll be there. I think too much of him not to be. Why can't he talk to his precious Chelsea? Actually, scrap that - I want to be the one he talks to. Always.

He walks away and I head towards my next lesson. That's when I hear them. Chelsea is standing by the lockers with a couple of her friends. They are surrounding Heidi and Sam. I don't have a good feeling about it – its as though they're trying to intimidate him. Sam has hung around with Chelsea a couple of times because he's been with me. He's not friends with her. In fact, I've noticed he seems to close down whenever she's near. Does anyone actually like Chelsea? Apart from Edward, that is.

"You have serious issues. Why don't you just face them instead of hanging around with Harper all the time."

My back stiffens. Chelsea is directing that to Sam. How dare she!

There are a few passers-by from lower years nosing as they walk past. Sam crosses his arms in front of himself as though protecting himself from her. My heart goes out to him and instinctively, I want to protect him.

"Why would you have a problem with me hanging with Harper?"

Chelsea narrows her eyes, "Because you're a coward, and I don't like cowards."

Huh, ironic, seeing as everyone that surrounds her, including me, are cowards.

Heidi speaks, "Come on, Chelsea, give him a break. There's no need for that."

"Oh, isn't there? I, for one, am getting rather tired of his presence."

"Why do you think I'm a coward?" His voice is shaking.

"You think we don't all know about you? Everyone knows but you're too much of a coward to come out and admit it. Why don't you just man up? Oh, wait a minute, you're not a man, are you?"

Heidi gasps, and that's it, I've heard enough.

Storming over, I shout. "You bitch!"

Anger consumes me. I can't even think straight. I don't even notice that half the school has gathered around and aren't hiding the fact that they're standing to watch the show.

"Harper, what the...?"

"How *dare* you talk to him like that!"

She sneers, "I'm doing you a favour."

"You are by far the worst person I have ever met. Why would you do this?" I am so mad, I have never felt like hitting anyone before, but I want to hit her so bad.

"Harper, what has got into you? Like you want him hanging around."

I glance at Sam. He looks like a deer caught in leadlights. He's never come out and said he's gay. It's his decision if and when he comes out. High school is hard enough, he should do it in his own time.

I see red that she's victimised him in this way.

I drop my bag on the floor and grab hold of her shoulders, pinning her to the wall. Everyone behind me gasps.

I lean into her face, so I'm only an inch away, "You are a vindictive evil witch. I would rather hang around with him anytime than hang with you? You know why... he's a nice guy and funny, two words you have absolutely no knowledge of."

Her eyes flash. "Piss off. You are showing your true colours, and you think I don't know what's going on with you and Edward."

I frown. What does she mean by that?

"Well, good luck... I've seen the way you drool over him. You have no chance - he sees you as the little girl next door and nothing else. You think you have a chance with him, you're so smug because you believe you know him better than anyone else. Well, he's into me because *I* know how to act with a guy."

She pushes me off her and straightens her top, regaining her composure. "By the way, at this school? You're done. I'll make sure that none of my friends give you the time of day. I'll make it so that people will be too scared to speak to you. You've just signed your popularity death warrant."

She sneers at me and turns to her friends, who have been silent this whole time, "Come on, leave these losers to it."

She turns and walks away. Whether or not her friends want to, they follow - they're sheep like I have been.

I turn to Sam, "Are you OK? I'm so sorry."

He shakes his head sadly, "I hate her."

Heidi goes over to him and hugs him. "Babe, ignore her. She will get her comeuppance, eventually."

I'm trembling from my outburst. I've never done anything like that before in my life.

Sam looks at us both. "Do you know what she was talking about?"

I shake my head. If he isn't ready to tell people he is gay, that's up to him. "No hun, don't take any notice of her. She's evil."

He nods and links us both. "Thank you, Harper. I know that you have just got yourself in a whole world of trouble for me.

You are amazing." He smiles at me.

"I couldn't see you treated that way—that has been a long time coming." I sigh.

We head to the next lesson together. What have I done?

My future at Arrowsmith High has just taken a whole new turn.

---

In the last lesson, I get a message from *Rookiewithgirls*. Does this guy actually do any work? I will read it on the way home.

*I needed time to think about my response to what you told me earlier.*

*I want you to listen to what I say carefully.* **You are special.** *You are beautiful inside and out, and no one, and I mean no one, not even your best friend, has a right to make you feel anything but the unique person you are.*

*I'm sorry that you heard your friend say that, is it possible that you were just kids, and it didn't mean anything, but you took it to heart and have been living your life by it since? You were kids. If he thought that years ago, chances are, he doesn't think that now. Popularity doesn't matter, you may believe it does, but it doesn't. Being true to yourself is the most important thing a person can do. Is that a hard thing to do in high school? Hell, yeah, it is, but nothing fantastic ever comes to you easily, right? Please listen to me when I say this - your good heart will shine through in everything you do. You do you, and you won't regret it. Don't let something some boy said years ago shape the person you are today. You will regret it if you aren't true to yourself.*

A tear rolls down my cheek as I read these words on the way to the bus. I wipe it away quickly so that no one sees. This guy knows me so well, he can see inside my mind. I needed those words today more than he could ever know. He's right. Now is the time where I should be brave. I need to figure out if I've got that in me. *Rookiewithgirls* is fast becoming my favourite person. Could Abraham be this sweet?

*Thank you. Your words are beautiful, and with the day I've had, I really needed to hear them.*

*No problem, I think it's time we meet, don't you?*

My stomach flips. I want to meet the guy that can get inside my head. Edward flashes through my mind - no one knows me like him, but he's not available and doesn't want me in that way, so I'd be stupid not to take my chance with *Rookiewithgirls*.

*Sure, let's do it.*

I leave it at that and put my phone away. I've been brave enough for one day. As I'm about to get on the bus, I hear someone calling my name behind me. I turn around, and Abraham is there, trying to catch up with me. This can't be a coincidence.

"Hey, Abe."

He smiles at me. He has a nice smile.

"Hey, are you free tonight? I was wondering if you fancied doing something? You know, just us." He scratches the back of his head and is finding it hard to meet my eye. This is it. This must be him, I've literally just finished messaging him about meeting, and he appears asking me out. Maybe he'll come clean about being *Rookiewithgirls*. This is it, the date I've been practising for, the kiss I've been practising for. My heart doesn't beat fast when I imagine kissing Abe, but I have to give it a go. All the things he's said in those emails, he knows me, cares for me, and thinks I'm beautiful inside and out and says that being popular isn't important - I wouldn't have thought that Abraham would think that, but just shows, you don't really know a person until you actually get to know them.

"That sounds nice. Yeah, I'd love to."

"Cool, can I call for you around seven? We could maybe walk into the village for ice cream?"

I nod, "Yeah that works for me."

He grins, "Brilliant, see you then."

So, I now have a date.

Rosie and Riley jump on the bus and come bounding towards me.

"Is it true? Please tell me it's true?"

They could be talking about anything - so much has happened today.

"If you mean did I pin Chelsea up against a wall and give up my life as I know it then, yeah, that was me."

Rosie and Riley scream and embrace me in a hug. "That is the best thing we've heard all month. You stood up to the She-bitch from hell! You are amazing. God, what was it like? Was it fantastic?"

"To be honest, I didn't even think about it. Now I feel sick and terrified."

"We heard Edward is gonna dump her."

My heart leaps. Is that true?

"Did you? Because of what happened?" I whisper.

"Who knows? Maybe not, maybe she'd heard that too, and that's why she was in such a foul mood and unfortunately took it out on Sam."

Is that why Edward was upset? Because he was going to end things with Chelsea. Surely it wouldn't bother him that much?

"Bloody hell, it's all happening today," I say in wonder.

Rosie speaks. "You know you did the right thing. We always wondered what you were doing hanging with her and her friends, you're so nice, and she's well... not."

I shrugged. "Popularity is important to me, I guess, or was - it's becoming less and less important to me every day, which is good because I am at the bottom of the food chain at the moment."

I tell them about my date with Abraham, but I can't stop wondering why Ed needed to talk to me.

## Chapter Seventeen

♥

Harper

So, this is it, my first actual date. Sadness washes over me that Edward doesn't even know.

It's nice out tonight, so I wear my fitted ripped jeans with my high wedges and team it with a light blue vest top. I do my hair down and wavy. I'm happy with the whole thing and know the top makes my blue eyes pop.

The butterflies are going crazy in my stomach. Maybe tonight, he'll tell me he is *Rookiewithgirls*. But if I have got it horribly wrong and he isn't *Rookiewithgirls*, that would mean that I'm going out with a guy that, honestly, I probably wouldn't have given a second glance to.

I scroll down my phone and click on Instagram to search around for a picture of him. I find one from one of Connor's parties. He is attractive, no question, he has sandy coloured hair and brown eyes. His personality has always been so loud - I would have entertained going out with him... until today.

I hear a knock at the door. Mum is out, as usual, so I make my way downstairs to answer.

Abraham is standing there when I open the door.

I smile at him. "Hey, I'm ready. I'll grab my bag."

*Deep breath Harper, you'll be fine.*

I go back to the door, "Hey, you look nice." He says to me.

I smile, "Thanks."

As we turn to walk down the street, I see Edward leaving his house. Damn! I didn't have time to tell him about Abraham. It's his fault anyway, he's the one that has stepped back from me. His eyes go to me and then Abe, giving him a chin lift.

He comes over, "Hey, what are you guys doing?"

Abe glances at me and back at Ed, "Dude, what's it look like? I've come to pick Harper up."

"What… like a date?"

He nods and slides his arm around my shoulders, making me stiffen. He's getting pretty familiar already. "Yeah, a date."

Edward's eyes drop to Abe's arm around my shoulders and his jaw clenches. What's with the sudden dislike of Abe?

He glares at me, "You never told me."

"No, I didn't get a chance. We arranged it after we talked today."

"Anyway dude, you're cramping my style. Catch up with ya later, yeah?"

Oh god, does anyone actually talk like that? I already doubt that it's *Rookiewithgirls* I'm with right now.

Ed backs away, "Sure, have fun, guys."

As we start walking, I shrug my shoulders to get him to drop his arm. No, thank you.

Things got even worse once we arrived at the Ice Cream Parlour. Now, I'm a modern girl, really, I am, but it's kind of gentlemanly for the guy to offer to pay. I have money and I was planning to do the whole '*What? No, don't be silly I'll pay for my own.*' routine, but he didn't even ask! He just got his own. It's a regular hang out for people at school and there are a few familiar faces around. We say hello to a couple. No doubt we will be the subject of gossip on Monday.

This is where it gets awkward. I have absolutely nothing to say to Abraham. He doesn't seem interested in making an effort.

This is going to be a painful night.

"So, what's your favourite subject at school?" he asks me.

Oh dear, I just want to be in the den with Ed right now. Why do things have to change?

I'm about to answer when the door opening catches my eye. My heart sinks. You have got to be kidding me. Why is he bringing her here? Seeing them both together makes bile rise in my throat. I can't believe that they're together. My blood is boiling.

He scans the room and stiffens when he sees us. He mutters something to Chelsea, I don't know what, but she shakes her head and walks to the counter. She hasn't seen me yet. He was probably trying to get her to leave.

She scans the room as she's waiting in line. Edward is still impersonating a statue at the door. Her eyes finally land on me and they narrow, assessing the situation and who I'm with, and she leaves the counter and comes marching over to me.

"Well, look who it is, didn't think you'd have the guts to show your face in here."

Edward is behind her in a flash, "Hey, what's going on?"

"Her." She points her finger at me in disgust. "Didn't you hear what she did to me?"

I sigh. I don't want to do this. "Chelsea, not now."

She leans forward and places her hands on the table, trying to lean over threateningly. I'm not scared of her—not anymore.

"What did you do to her?" Edward is frowning.

"Yeah, I wanna know too." Abe says

"It was nothing."

"Oh, you mean, pinning me by my throat against the lockers was nothing? I thought you were going to choke me."

Edwards's eyes widen, "You did *what?*"

I can't blame him for not believing it. I don't believe I did it either. That's the first time I've ever truly lost my temper, but God, did she deserve it.

"Yeah, your girlfriend here was saying mean things about my friend. What can I say? I lost my temper."

"She's not my girlfriend."

Chelsea straightens and spins around to glare at Edward.

Which friend?" Ed asks

"Sam," I say to him, realisation dawns over him. He realises what she would have said to Sam. His face hardens. "You were mean to Sam?"

She shrugs, "Well, I was trying to get him to come to terms with something that he should have done a while ago."

"What should he have come to terms with?" Abraham asks.

"That-"

I cut her off. No way is she making Sam the talk of the school. I stand quickly, "Don't you dare, Chelsea."

"Oo, going to attack me again, are you?"

Ed grabs her arm and steers her towards the door, "We're going."

"But we just got here."

"Yeah, we need to talk."

He ushers her out without another word.

I sit back down and turn to Abe, "Sorry about that."

"So, you stood up to Chelsea? Didn't know any girl had the guts to do that."

I smile, "Yeah well, you can only be pushed so far, right?"

He grins, "Obviously. You get more and more interesting."

"Aren't you bothered? That I'm now a social pariah?"

He shakes his head, "Nah, couldn't care less about that stuff."

How weird that the most popular guys are the ones saying they don't care about being popular, doesn't seem fair.

The date goes a lot better after that. Chelsea being evil apparently lightened the mood. We chat about what movies we like and what we like to do. He doesn't mention *Rookiewithgirls*. The more I talk with him, the more I know for sure that there's no way that he is my secret admirer. Without sounding mean, I don't believe he would have the foresight to do something like that. He doesn't seem to have any imagination. But the date is pleasant, and we decide to go for a walk after ice cream, then he said he'd take me home.

As we walk, he takes hold of my hand, and I let him. I remember how exciting it felt with Edward, maybe because I know Ed inside out, and I'm comfortable with him. Or perhaps something different entirely.

I wonder what happened with Chelsea and Edward. Are they over now? I'm dying to know. I can't check on Instagram as Chelsea and her friends have blocked me, and Edward would never go on Instagram. I'm going to have to find out from him tomorrow.

When we are a little way from my house, he pulls me to a stop near some trees. My stomach flips. I know why he's stopped me. He's going to kiss me. This is what the practice has been about - I know what I'm doing now, right? So I should go for it.

I glance at him, "Hey, why have we stopped?"

"I've had a good time tonight."

"Yeah, it was good."

"I'd like to do it again."

I tilt my head. "Would you?"

"Yeah, and I'd like to kiss you."

Why does this feel so wrong? I'm not excited.

He leans his head in to give me a peck and places his hands on my waist as though he's going to go in for a longer kiss. It's in that moment that I realise I can't do it. I don't want to. This is nothing like it was with Ed.

I don't feel anything for him, you know why? My world spins as I realise something - I have feelings for my best friend.

## Chapter Eighteen

Harper

"I'm sorry, Abraham, I can't. You're nice and all, but I'm sorry it's just not there."

He steps back. "I thought we had fun tonight."

"What if I said to you that you were a rookie with girls?"

His eyes widen, "What the hell? No I'm not."

That confirms it - he isn't *Rookiewithgirls*. I figured that out in the first five minutes of our date anyway, so that leaves the question who the heck is *Rookiewithgirls*?

I shake my head. "No, I'm sorry, of course you're not. I was seeing if you knew the code for something."

He frowns, now clearly disgruntled. "What are you talking about?"

I can't help but let out a little chuckle at his confused face. He doesn't know whether to be aggravated or confused.

"Sorry Abraham, can we call quits on tonight? Thank you for taking me out, but I'm pretty sure I like someone else."

He sighs and puts his hands in his pockets. "It's Edward, isn't it?"

"What? No! Why would you say that?"

He shakes his head, "Forget it. OK, let's get you home." He says sadly.

This now leaves me in a right mess. I don't know who *Rookiewithgirls is,* and now I think I have feelings for my best friend. Why was kissing him so amazing? It felt so right. Oh god, getting feelings for him is the last thing I want to do. How did it even happen?

I should swear off boys altogether. I'm obviously not a natural at this kind of stuff.

I go upstairs, get into my pyjamas and plonk myself on my bed. My phone buzzes.

It's mum. **Staying out with Derek tonight, things OK there?** She does not know what's going on in my life at all.

**Yeah, all good. See you in the morning.**

I know full well I won't see her in the morning, because she won't be back in time before I go to school.

I need to get out of here. I want to be in the den. It's the only place I can relax these days. Should I go in there without Ed, though? Probably not, but it's safe. No one has ever been in those woods, ever.

Sod it, I'm going, I'm in here on my own anyway, might as well sleep in there.

I grab my laptop and phone for if I want to watch a movie and walk through the garden. I spend ten minutes there, nipping a few dead heads off, pulling a few weeds, and putting them in the green recycling bin… so satisfying.

I climb in and scan around. All my memories of Edward and I are in here from being young. The rockets we made at preschool, the pumpkin pictures, the shell sculptures we made at the lake house, so much, and many happy times. How did I end up looking at him differently? What makes someone go from friends to something more? It has totally crept up on me. I hate that he's with Chelsea, and seeing them together drives me crazy.

Maybe I'll find out tomorrow that their relationship has come to an abrupt end. Hopefully.

*Rookiewithgirls*. Who could it be? I wish it would be Edward– that he liked me too. That kiss was intense, so perfect - it would make everything slip into place. Unfortunately, life isn't like that.

I switch on my laptop. Nothing from *Rookiewithgirls,* and I don't want to message him right now, I'm too confused. I search through Netflix and decide on New Girl that I started watching last week. I lie back and watch some TV.

Timeout to collect my thoughts is what I need. Then I need to run away to a foreign country.

# Chapter Nineteen

♥

Edward

I watch through the window like a nosey neighbour as she says goodbye to Abraham. OK, so no action there, no kiss, no handholding. I relax my shoulders and exhale. Thank God.

I check my phone, contemplating if I should message her, as me, not *Rookiewithgirls*. I hate how we are with each other at the moment, everyone knew us as a duo… inseparable, and now, because of others coming into the mix, it's all falling apart.

Should I tell her I'm *Rookiewithgirls*? I need to speak to her about what she said. It cuts me in half that she overheard me talking about her like that. Why didn't she tell me? She's kept it to herself all these years. I hurt her - I *hate* that I hurt her.

It's that kiss. It changed everything. Maybe it shouldn't have happened, but it was the best thing that has ever happened.

There's some noise at the back of the house. I check it out and see Harper make her way through the garden. Of course she fiddles with some plants and makes her way out the back gate. Why is she going to the den? Weird.

I should talk to her, make things right with her.

I make us some hot chocolate and grab some crisps and a pack of biscuits from the cupboard. I put it all on a tray and open the back door.

"Where are you going?" Dad asks. He points to the tray. "The den? It's a little late, isn't it?"

"I think Harper might be upset. I saw her go in there and want to check she's OK."

"Have you two got some issues at the moment? I've noticed she hasn't been around as much."

"Kinda, Dad, but it's my fault."

He nods. "She's a good girl - you'll take care of her, won't you?"

I frown at him, "Of course."

"She doesn't have her dad much around anymore. I've sort of taken over that role. Don't think I haven't seen the way you look at her now."

"It's... I don't know, Dad, it's complicated."

"It always is son, just be careful with her feelings and look after her."

I nod, "I'm trying my best."

He pats me on the shoulder and walks out.

Does everyone in the world know I have feelings for Harper?

It's a warm night. I make my way through our garden, where the tulips and daffodils are in bloom that Harper planted for us. As I walk to the den, I get nervous. I don't know what I'm going to say. I have nothing planned.

She's lying on her stomach, watching her laptop with her earphones in. She has no idea I'm there. Not safe at all. I put the tray down and nudge her leg.

She spins around, her earbuds falling out. "Jesus Cap, you scared the living hell out of me."

I raise my eyebrows, "Is it a good idea to lie here with earbuds in? You didn't even hear me come in."

She waves her hand in dismissal. "No one ever comes here. It's fine."

"No, you shouldn't be out here on your own."

"In all the years of us coming here, have you ever seen one living soul other than our parents and Coop?" She crosses her arms waiting for my answer.

"Well... no, but there's always a first time."

"What are you doing out here, anyway?"

She shrugs and turns away, "I wanted to hang in here."

I stare at her until she's forced to meet my gaze. I know she only comes in here to either hang with me or when she's worried or upset about something.

She sighs. "Fine. I had a terrible night to top off the worst day ever, and Mum isn't around, as per usual."

"Why didn't you text me?"

Her eyes meet mine and they so full of sadness it's like a knife to the gut. "Didn't seem right at the moment."

"We need to have a chat. Here," I hand her the hot chocolate. "we need to sort this out."

"Sort what out?"

"Us. Things have been weird between us, and they've never been weird. I hate it."

She sighs and her shoulders droop, "Me too. It's like we're drifting apart or something."

"I never wanted that to happen. I *never* want that to happen ever."

"Did Chelsea give you the full story about what happened with her and Sam today?"

"Yeah, reading between the lines, I'm guessing she was a bitch with Sam."

"Yup, I couldn't let her treat him that way. I signed my death warrant, didn't I?"

"You defended your friend. You have nothing to regret - you absolutely did the right thing."

"I proper lost it, though."

"Yeah, with good reason."

"So much for being popular, huh?"

"Not this again. How many times do we have to go over this again and again? Being popular means nothing - it's not important."

He gives a bitter laugh. "Says the guy who's one of the most popular and been going out with the girl who is the most popular. You keep preaching this to me, but you don't practice it, do you?"

She is so frustrating! "I can't help being popular. I don't try."

"Well, bully for you."

"I didn't mean it like that, and I can explain the Chelsea thing."

She tilts her head to one side after taking a drink of the hot chocolate. "There isn't anything to explain. She's pretty and popular."

"I like someone else."

She sits up straight, paying attention now.

"Do you?"

"Yeah, maybe I was trying to get her attention, *maybe* I was trying to make her jealous. It was a stupid thing to do, it was Jasper's idea and it well and truly backfired on me."

"You did *what*? Jasper is an idiot, then. Why did you listen to him?"

I give a half-laugh, "I have absolutely no idea."

"Did it work? Did she get jealous?"

It's now or never. I should say something now, ask her if she was jealous. Oh god, I'm sweating. I can't do this. Yup, I have to, it's now or never.

"Well, I don't know..." I was going to say something I was, but then I thought about how awkward it would be if she didn't like me like that... and that would be it, we'd never be friends again. So yeah... I chickened out... again.

I need to man up, but tonight is not the night.

"You know what, I have no idea, I don't know what I'm doing, I know nothing about the opposite sex. There you go, I admitted it."

She gives a half-laugh. "Join the club."

I take this opportunity to change the subject, "So... date with Abraham, huh? How did that work out? Seeing as you're in here moping about your bad day, I'm guessing it didn't go too well."

"You guessed right, it just wasn't there. There is no way he is *Rookiewithgirls.*, He was nice enough, and it made me realise I shouldn't judge people. I always presumed he was a nightmare, but he wasn't. But I don't like him in that way, and he kissed me and..."

"*What*? When?"

"Right before he brought me home, anyway, I wasn't feeling it, so I pulled away after a peck."

"So, you didn't get to try out your new experience?"

She shakes her head and gives me a small smile, "No, you're still the only one that gets that."

Warmth floods my body. I'm the only one that's ever kissed her.

She shrugs and carries on, "Anyway, I still have *Rookiewithgirls*, right? Things are weird there too."

"Why would you say that?"

"I opened up to him about stuff and am scared that I said too much. What if I can't trust him?"

I don't walk to talk about *Rookiewithgirls*. That's another mess I've got myself into.

"I'm sure if he was going to be nasty or do something underhand, he would have done it by now."

She shakes her head, "You know what? I'm pissed off at him. He's the one that caused me to go on that stupid date with someone I didn't like because I thought it might be him. He's a coward. He should have made himself known by now. Actually, I'm super pissed off at him. I might tell him, or I might just block him. I'm done. He likes me, he should have the balls to come forward and tell me."

This is not going well at all. "Wow, you are not happy, are you?"

She flops down on the sleeping back, "No, stupid guys, making my life a misery, playing with me. I'm done. He comes to me now he can get lost."

"Harp, it can't be that bad. Maybe he's a decent guy who's scared of rejection."

She rolls her eyes, "Come on, can you imagine ever doing anything so lame to get a girl. No, he's playing with me."

Does she have any idea at all how hard all this is for me? I didn't mean to fall in love with my best friend! I give up. "Whatever, sometimes I wonder if you even know what you want."

"What do you mean by that?"

"Come on, Harp, you know what I mean. You want to be popular, or you think you do, but you don't like any of the girls you hang with. You want to do something you love but don't have the guts. Guys are shallow, right? That's what you're always telling me, but one tries to know you on a different level, and you shut him down. Do you actually know at this point?"

"How can you say that to me? You know me inside out." Her voice sounds shaky, but I don't take that cue and I carry on. "Do I, though? You're so complicated when everything could be so easy."

"Argh, I'm under so much pressure. Don't be mad at me. Like I said, I don't know what I'm doing anymore."

I sigh and slide my arm around her, pulling her to me, and she relaxes. I whisper into her hair, "I know, Buttercup, but you'll see, there's no need to put all this pressure on yourself."

"You believe that because you're... well... you. I'm not all that, so I need to work at it."

I can't help it, I kiss the top of her head, "That's the stupidest thing I've ever heard."

Her body gets more relaxed in my arms, "I always feel so safe, so comfortable when I'm with you."

*Yeah, me too, and a whole lot more.*

This girl is it for me. After a moment's silence, I whisper, "I think the world of you, you know." I release her. Things are getting way too intense. "Come on, let's watch a movie but then promise me you'll go back to bed in your room."

She sighs, "OK, I promise."

We settle down to watch *17 Again*—I let her pick, and apparently, she's in the mood for Zack Effron.

## Chapter Twenty

♥

Harper

**Can you meet me before registration?**

I frown, a message from Sam. Hope he's OK after yesterday. I care about him, we've become such good friends. I messaged him after the Chelsea thing, and he said he was out with his brother and he would call me, but I never got a call.

I reply; **Sure, on the bus now. Meet you in five.**

Edward sees my face, "What's up?"

I shrug, "Sam wants me before we go in."

He gives a slight nod and starts chatting to the others.

We arrive five minutes early, so I head over to registration, hoping Sam will already be there. He is, and he's looking around and figiting.

"Hey, what's the matter?"

His whole body relaxes when he spots me. "Thank goodness you're here. I need to talk to you." He looks around and grabs my hand, walking around the corner where there is a lot less student traffic.

"You're scaring me. Is this about yesterday?"

He shakes his head, "I'm OK, sort of. I need to tell you something before the entire school starts talking about me."

Oh god, what has he done?

"Okay."

"We're friends, right?"

I nod slowly, "Unless you're a serial killer, then yes."

He half laughs, obviously not finding me funny at all. "OK, let me get this out."

I wait as he takes a deep breath and closes his eyes. He opens them slowly. "I'm gay."

I wait for something further, nothing. "Yeah, so? Is that it?"

He stares at me, stunned. "Yes, that's it."

"Wait, that's the big news you wanted to tell me?"

"Well, yeah."

I laugh, "Babe, I know, I presumed you knew I knew. It's not a big deal, is it?"

His eyes widen. "Yes! It's an enormous deal. Do you realise what I've been going through, how much courage I've had to pluck up to tell you? I had a serious conversation with my brother last night and got the reaction you have had. He says I should come out, tell everyone."

"And you don't?"

He runs his hands through his hair and sighs, "I don't know. After talking to my brother, my head is in a better place, and now I've told you, that kind of feels good, even though I seem to have got worked up over nothing. Maybe I should just do it."

"Aw Sam, I'm so happy that you spoke to your brother and me - it must have taken real courage. I know it can't be easy, being a teenage boy with these emotions, but you know what? I'm pretty sure most people have figured it out on their own or have their suspicions, anyway."

"Yeah, I know, I give off that vibe, right? I know I'm a bit lacking in testosterone."

I chuckle, "Yeah, but trust me, that's not a bad thing."

He leans back against the wall, looking a little more relaxed. "Should I do it?"

"You're the only one that can make that decision, it's a big one, but I'll be right behind you if you do, and Heidi and Anna and Ed. We all will."

He leans in and gives me a hug as the bell goes. "You're the best."

At the end of registration, he walks with me to my next lesson. "I'm going to do it. If people act like you and my brother, it'll all be good.

I grimace, "Yeah, I can't promise that. You know there are horrible people here too, but I guess that's life, right? Not everyone can be nice."

He frowns, "Can I ask something?"

"Sure."

"Well, you're so nice to everyone, but yet you hang with all the girls that are *not* nice and seem to kinda hang on their every word. Why do you do that?"

"Not you too." I roll my eyes.

"How do you mean?"

"Ed keeps having digs at me for hanging with them."

"So why do you?"

I hate being put on the spot like this. How do I explain? "It's a long story."

"Maybe we could hang out one night, and you can explain it to me."

I smile. If he's got the guts to do this, then I've certainly got the guts to be open with him. "I'd like that. I'm free tonight?"

He grins, "Excellent, we could go to Nando's?"

I nod, "Sounds like a plan. So, how you gonna do all this coming out thing?"

He grins at me, "Well... that's where you come in."

"Me?"

"Yeah, maybe you could drop the info to your friends? I'm not using you I swear, but you know everyone, and you could maybe make sure a certain person gets hold of the info. I know you two aren't exactly best buddies at the moment, but I'm sure you know how to get the info to her. So I don't have to make an announcement in assembly or anything. She's just as efficient as an assembly."

I nod, "She sure is, and yeah, I don't mind. I'll tell some of her acquaintances at lunch, it'll be all around the school by last break."

We walk into the class together, and he gives me a peck on the cheek. "You're the best."

I love him, I do. I'm so glad I met him. It's a whole different friendship than the one I have, well had, with Edward, and this one will never get blurred like the one Edward's and mine seem to be getting.

---

I was right. By the end of the last break, everyone in our year knew that Sam had come out. Good job I wasn't trusting these people with my gossip, eh? Like I ever would. The reaction was as I thought. Most decent people either acted like it was no big deal - which it wasn't - the others, of course, were mean about it, just for the chance to be mean. It takes real guts to do what he's done.

I scan the courtyard for Sam but can't see him anywhere. I hope he's OK, out of the corner of my eye I see someone rushing towards me.

It's Ed.

I smile at him. "Hey, Cap."

He has a face like thunder. "Please tell me it isn't true."

"Oh god, what have I done now?"

"Sam - you didn't spread that around school, did you? Please tell me you didn't."

Now I get mad. How could he possibly believe I would do that? Does he know me at all?

"No, and it pisses me off that you think I would do that."

"Well, Jasper told me, and he heard it from Chelsea, who apparently is telling everyone that you started the rumour, and you guys are friends. Or I thought you were."

"Well, get down of your high horse and find out from me before you hear. Jesus Edward, what's happening to us?"

He frowns and shakes his head, "You'll do anything to be in with Chelsea, no matter what she's like or who she hurts."

I gasp. Does he really believe that?

"I'll tell you what. If you think that, why are we even friends?"

"Well, tell me you didn't do it."

I could do, I could straighten this out right here, but why should I? He's being horrible to me, and it hurts so much that he believes I'm capable of that. He knows me. Is this what everyone thinks of me, that I would sell my soul to the devil if it meant getting what I want. Sam is the sweetest, nicest guy I know, and he thinks I would screw him over.

"Piss off Edward. Go hang out with decent people, the opposite of me."

I turn around and walk away, fighting the tears that are threatening to fall. Every emotion is rushing through me right now, anger, hurt, betrayal, everything I thought about me and Edward, how solid we were, what a joke that was, God if you asked me this time 6 months ago, or a year ago, I would say nothing would rock us. And how stupid am I? Because not only does he think so little of me as a friend, but now I have gone and gotten feelings for him, so it hurts twice as much.

Silly, *silly* girl.

## Chapter Twenty-one

♥

Harper

I don't get the bus home after school. I'm so upset with Edward, and I don't want Coop or all the others to see me.

How ironic that the one place I felt I could be myself, on the school bus with the friends I have there, is now the place I can't go.

I message Sam. **Hey, do you still want to meet tonight?**

I didn't see him the rest of the day, so I don't know how things went for him.

My phone pings in reply, **Of course. What time?**

**As soon as possible?**

**Sure, but we don't know our way around yet, can I get my brother to bring me to yours and we can go to Nando's, my treat?**

I smile. **Sounds good, but I'll pay my half, honey.**

**I owe you big time for today so I'm paying.**

I text back. **We will talk about that later. What time?**

**Five?**

**Perfect.**

I message Mum to come and get me, but of course, she isn't available. Great. It's about a half-hour walk. Best get walking.

Placing my earphones in, I set off, only playing the happiest songs so that I can pretend that my world isn't falling apart.

A car arrives with Sam in the passenger seat so I make my way out. Edward hasn't been in touch, so he obviously thinks I did spread Sam's rumour for my own personal gain.

The empty hollow feeling in my stomach feels like it's getting bigger and bigger, eating away at me.

I leave the house and wave at Sam. He gets out to let me in the back seat.

"Hey gorgeous, this is my brother, Max."

I climb inside, "Hey Max, nice to meet you."

He smiles at me warmly, "Yeah you too. Good to hear my brother has made a good friend here so soon."

"Yeah, I love him - he's great."

He smiles warmly, "Well, I wouldn't go that far."

He turns back to the road and glances at Sam. "OK, Nando's right." His eyes meet mine through the mirror. "We're not overly familiar with the area yet. Is that on the retail park?"

I nod, "Yeah, next to the cinema."

He nods and sets off driving.

Once we've ordered our food and our drinks have come, I turn my attention to Sam. "So, how was the rest of the day."

He grimaces, "Good, I guess, a lot of people were looking, a couple of guys said something to me, two girls even came over and said well done blah blah, but then the pastoral head, Mrs Swindell, came over and said she wanted to see me. She told me she had heard about me and wanted to check I was OK and asked if there was anything she could do."

"Oh my god, did she know that you had intended it to come out?"

"Not at first. She thought it had come out by accident, so she was a lot happier when I told her that was my intention. She was super nice actually, said that her door is always open for me if I need her."

"Big few weeks for you, moving to a new place, starting a new school, and now coming out as gay. Wow, you have got to be the bravest guy I have ever met. I'm so proud of you."

"If I hadn't met you and got on so well, I wouldn't have had the guts to do it, but knowing you had my back, well, it's a massive thing."

I shrug, "You should do you and stuff what everyone else thinks. Who you are is absolutely brilliant, and I'm glad you've realised that too."

He stares at me.

"What?"

"Do you hear yourself?"

I shake my head, "I don't get it."

"Babe, all you say to me is that I should stand tall, be myself - love myself for who I am - when here you are walking around behaving exactly the opposite."

"No I'm not. I'm doing what normal teenage girls do - trying to figure myself out and trying to fit in."

"But don't you see how amazing you are?"

I shake my head, "I'm really not. I... well, I hide stuff, I'm not nearly as cool as I make out."

"Being mainstream isn't cool, Harper. I mean, it is, if that's who you want to be, but I think that you're being who you think everyone wants you to be."

"I know what guys like. I just want to be loved by someone. Everyone wants that, right?"

"Why would you think guys like girls who are fake?"

I sigh, he trusted me with the most important thing in his life, so I should trust him. "OK, so, for this, I have to start at the beginning."

"Thank god. Continue." He leans back in his chair.

"When I was 10, I had a massive crush on Edward."

"I totally get that. I bet he was even hot at eleven."

"Oh wait, I have to tell you the most important thing." I look around to check no one can hear, and Sam leans in, obviously presuming he was going to get the juice of the century. I whisper, "I like gardening."

He frowns, "What does that mean?"

My turn to frown, "What does that mean? What do you think it means? I like to spend time in the garden, with plants and stuff, gardening."

"I am totally confused right now. One, why are you bringing that up right now, random fact about you, but two, why are you whispering it as though you told me you like to dance naked around Manchester at night."

I laugh. He has a point, I *am* being a little dramatic. "OK, so I've always loved gardening, people read to escape or watch a movie, but from being little, all I've ever wanted was to be in the garden. I can name every plant, flower, tell you about acidity in soil, you name it, I know it. I've designed most of the gardens in my street and a few others besides."

"So gardening is your thing, I get it. But why the secret?"

"Because it's not cool - it is so the opposite of cool that I have a problem saying it out loud."

"Cool is what you make it, baby girl."

"I wish I had your philosophy, but I do not. Anyway, so Ed always knew this about me, we grew up next to each other, friends since we were toddlers, so he just takes me as is. Or so I thought. I had this dream when I was 10 that we were going to fall in love and get married; blah blah, don't ask me the details, I didn't have any, I just presumed that was what would happen. We're naïve when we're 10, right?"

"So I'm guessing Edward did something to upset the balance?"

"Yeah, I overheard him talking with a friend when he started high school. The guy asked him about me and he laughed and said that no way would he ever go for a girl like me, that boys don't like tomboys, they like girlie girls that are feminine - that girls with dirt up her fingernails is not his cup of tea."

Sam puts his hands on mine, "I'm so sorry, sweetie, that must have been awful for you to overhear, were you devastated?"

I nod, "I was, at first, but I decided that Edward knew me best of all, so that if he would not want to be with me, then no one would. I decided I had to change my ways. Be that girl that he said all guys like, so I've always kept the gardening thing a secret."

"Did your relationship with Edward suffer?"

I shrug as I try to recall, "Maybe a little for a week or so, then I shut out of my mind any kind of crush and accepted him for what he is, was, or whatever, my best friend."

"This is a lot of drama for you to deal with when your 10."

I chuckle, "Same as any other 10-year-old I imagine that likes a boy."

"So let me get this straight. You liked Edward. You heard him say something when he was ELEVEN." He slowly pronounced the word eleven, "and decided to live the rest of your life by it."

When he puts it like that, it sounds idiotic. "I guess."

"I'm not sure where to start. First of all, you like what you like. This is all rubbish. You heard a kid say this to another kid. Have you ever asked him about this?"

I shake my head, "No, what's the point? He'd only deny it?"

"Well yeah, cos he's 17 and knows that's not true anymore. Christ, he hadn't even gone through puberty."

"Trust me, as the years have gone on, I've seen what guys like, and he was right."

"Well, maybe some. I can't speak for straight guys, can I? But it all depends, do you care what other guys want, or do you care what Edward wants? Because I've seen the way he looks at you. I'm not sure it's all friendship on his part."

I roll my eyes, "You're not the first person to say that, but trust me, he doesn't see me that way."

I flashback to that fantastic kiss, it was intense, but more so for me than him, I'm sure.

My phone rings. I check the display, it's a local number but one I don't recognise, I answer it.

"Hello?"

"Hello, am I speaking to Miss Lloyd?"

I frown, "You are, and who is this please?"

"This is Brenda Gibson."

I stiffen, no way. This is the competition. Brenda Gibson is the owner of the estate. Sam notices my reaction and mouths, "Who is it?"

"Oh, er, hello, Mrs Gibson."

"Brenda, please. I'm so happy to speak to you, young lady. I'd like to talk to you about your competition entry."

"Nice to speak to you too."

"It will be even nicer in a minute, as I'm pleased to tell you, you won."

I catch my breath, and my hand flies to my chest, "I won?"

"You were by far the most talented and original. I loved your proposal right from the beginning. The fact that you are a young lady at high school absolutely astounds me, if you're this good now, in a few years you will take the world by storm."

"Oh my goodness, I don't know what to say. Thank you, thank you so much."

"Can we meet? I have a local newspaper waiting to hear from me, they want to interview us both for the article, they couldn't believe how old you were and the level of expertise you have and want to know all about you. You will be quite a celebrity around here."

My stomach sinks down to my toes. Oh god. I'd be in the paper, everyone would see, my secret would be out.

I need to get off this phone call. I need to get my thoughts together.

"Yes, of course, that would be good. Do you think I could call you back tomorrow? I am in the middle of dinner with a friend in a restaurant. I could call you back tomorrow evening after school?"

"Of course, my dear, that will be fine. Sorry I didn't mean to disturb you. I just thought you'd want to know that you won as soon as possible. You will have to think about what you want to do with the prize money."

I nod numbly, then realise I have to speak. "Yes, I certainly will, and I appreciate you calling me, I'm stuck for words. Thank you so much, Mrs Gibson."

"No, thank you, I'm going to have the nicest garden in Manchester, if not England."

We say our goodbyes and end the call - I stare at Sam.

"Are you going to tell me what that was all about?"

I slam my phone down on the table. "I'm not sure if the best thing or the worst thing has just happened to me."

I tell him about the competition and how much of a big deal it is, then I tell him about the phone conversation.

"This is great. I'm so happy for you."

"Yeah, it's such a great opportunity, and the prize, I mean, 50k, jeez, mum and I, we get by, but we don't have loads of money since dad left, and that would be great for Uni. I just..." I sigh and shake my head.

Sam answers, "You don't want to be in the paper. You don't want anyone to know your dirty little secret."

I nod, "Yeah, and believe me, I realise how shallow that makes me sound."

"Yeah it does, and you're not shallow. Honestly, Harper, I want to shake you sometimes."

"Gee, thanks."

He grabs my hand again. "Listen, you have to learn to be you. No matter what. If you can't be true to yourself in this life, what's the point? Do what you love, or you'll never be happy, and don't let the comments of a child rule your life forever. Are you really going to turn down an opportunity of a lifetime because of what the other kids at school will say. You're the one that backed me to be me, so now I'm going to back you being you."

I sigh, "I need to think about it. Can we pay and head home?"

He stares at me for a moment. "Sure, but follow your heart, and for god's sake, talk to Edward about what you heard because I'm pretty sure that he can make you see clearly."

As I get into bed that night, I go over what Sam said, about what Edward has told me many times. Can I do this? Can I be brave and just be who I am, forget Chelsea and trying to please her all the time? Hang with who I want to hang with and if I want to be scruffy one day, I can be, or not wear make-up, or be in the paper for my gardening expertise. The thought of doing this makes me want to be sick.

I get a text from Sam. **Being afraid is good. It means you want something badly, night, love you.**

God, I love him.

## Chapter Twenty-Two

♥

Edward

My phone rings and I check the time, 10pm, can only be Harp. 'unknown caller'.

"Hello?"

"Hi Edward, this is Sam, Harper's friend. Can we talk? It's important."

I sit up in bed, "Is she OK?"

He sighs, "Yeah, well actually, no."

"What's the matter with her." Fear clutches my insides.

"She won."

"What?"

"The competition, she won, she found out tonight, while we were at Nando's together."

Go, Harper.

"That's amazing. I knew she would knock it out of the park. She's amazing. I'm glad she's told you about that. She doesn't tell many people, she must trust you."

Why do I hate that she's let someone else into her trust circle? I should be happy because I sure as hell haven't been there for her lately, but I hate it.

"Yeah, she does. I trusted her with something important, and we bonded."

"Wait, so she didn't tell spread gossip about you?"

"Oh yeah, she did, because I asked her to. I wanted to come out, I thought the quickest way for everyone to find out would be if Chelsea found out. I may have not been at this school long, but I can tell that she acts like the queen bee."

Oh god, what have I done? I groan.

"What?"

"Well, Harp and I aren't speaking at the moment. I kind of accused her of being a bitch. I thought she'd told everyone about you for the sake of being the one in the know, with the gossip."

"Oh Edward, how could you think that of her?"

I shake my head, "I don't know, I have no idea what's going on with us, everything we've had for years, it's going down the drain. The more I try with her, the more I seem to mess up."

"You like her, don't you?"

"Of course I do. We've been best friends since we were two."

"That's not what I mean."

I close my eyes tight. Should I confide in him? He is betraying Harper right now, but because he cares for her.

"Yeah, alright, yeah, I do."

"I knew it."

"Does she, has she... said anything about me?"

"No, but she's not happy that you two aren't good, and honestly, she might not have said anything, but I have my doubts that it's purely platonic for her too."

"Has she told you about *Rookiewithgirls*?"

"She did. She's kind of dismissed him now."

"Yeah, that was a stupid idea of mine too."

"*That was you*?"

"Fraid so."

"Oh my god, what are you two like? Why don't you just sit down and have an honest conversation."

"Yeah, we're about due. Anyway, we've got off-topic. What's wrong with her? Isn't she happy?"

"Well, yeah, until she found out that she has to be interviewed in the local paper and now she's contemplating turning it down because she doesn't want everyone to know."

"What, that is so screwed up. I mean, typically Harper, but I can't believe she'd turn it down because of her image."

"That's why I'm phoning you. She will kill me if she finds out that I'm telling you this, but you have to know."

My stomach clenches again. What isn't she telling me?

He relays the information I already know about her overhearing me, but he tells me about how it affects her today, and a lot of that conversation is ingrained into her and makes her like she is today.

I'm quiet for a little too long as I process this.

"You still there, Edward?"

"Yeah, I am. I know about the conversation she overheard."

"Why haven't you said anything to her?" he asks quietly.

"Because she told someone that in confidence, and I can't break that confidence." Meaning *Rookiewithgirls,* who is, of course, me. How have I messed this up so much? Starting those letters was the stupidest thing I have ever done.

"Well, I'm sorry, but whoever it is, I'm sure they wouldn't mind if they knew how much it affected her. It's time to break that confidence. Think about it."

"OK, Sam. And thanks, thanks for getting in touch with me about this. I care about her, you know."

"Yeah, I can see that. I'll leave you to it. See you at school tomorrow."

I lie back down in bed and wonder how the hell she can even think about turning down the competition. There are only so many times that you can tell someone that she can just be herself. She won't listen. How can I get her to believe it?

She's my first thought as I wake this morning, I need to speak to her. We did not leave things great last night. In fact, they were downright awful. Will she even talk to me?

I get ready early and wait at the window, watching for her to leave to go to the bus stop. I don't hear Cooper creep up behind me. He leans in and says right next to my ear, "stalking is an offence, you know."

"Jesus, you stupid git! You frightened me to death."

He throws his head back and laughs, "seriously funny, though."

"I'm waiting for Harper to come out. I need to talk to her."

"Still not sorting things out with her, huh?"

I shake my head, "no, will you hang back while I walk to the bus with her? I need to talk to her."

He nods, "I will, but if you two don't sort your mess out soon, I will sort it out for you."

I frown, "what does that mean."

He shrugs and waggles his eyebrows, "you don't want to find out." He backs away and walks into the kitchen. Arse.

I see her walk down the path and grab my backpack, rushing out to catch up with her.

"Harper, wait."

She stops and turns around but then seems to remember she's not speaking to me and turns around and carries on.

I touch her arm when I'm by her side. "We need to talk."

"No we don't."

"I'm sorry about what I said. I should have known you would never do that. I cant believe I I doubted you. I'm so sorry, Buttercup. Please don't fall out with me."

She stops walking and spins around to face me. "Finally found out the truth did you? Well, too little too late, how could you, after everything. All those years of being friends, you don't know me at all."

"Well, do you blame me? I mean, come on, sometimes it seems as though you would do anything to please those guys."

She narrows her eyes at me, "So you still have this low opinion of me, I see."

"From what I heard last night, your decisions are getting more and more stupid."

"What the hell is that supposed to mean?"

"The competition, I know you won, and that you're thinking of turning it down because you'll be a local celebrity or whatever."

Her mouth drops open, "Sam... Sam told you?"

I calm myself down a little, getting wound up is getting us nowhere, "he did. I'm sorry, don't be mad at him, he's worried about you and thought you might turn it down for the wrong reasons."

"And what reasons would those be?"

"We need to talk."

"You've made the way you feel about me perfectly clear. See you around, Edward."

"Fine, you don't want to talk, suit yourself, but I'll tell you this, if you turn this down, it will be the stupidest decision you will ever make. It's about time you grow up and be who you want to be instead of all this high school crap! If you turn this down, you are not the person I thought you were."

I see tears in her eyes as she turns and walks away. That went a hundred times worse than I expected. I need to fix this, fix us, before it's too late.

She needs to figure this out herself. When she does, whatever she decides, she needs to know that she's got me rooting for her and not against her.

Great job, Edward.

## Chapter Twenty-Three

♥

Harper

I hate him. Well, ironically, I love him. But I also hate him.

He is being so mean to me, and Sam? I can't believe he ran straight to Edward and told him, I thought he was my friend.

I tossed and turned all night, trying to decide what to do. Bottom line? I know exactly what I want to do but I don't know if I have the guts to do it, to finally say 'good riddance' to Chelsea, to caring about being popular, caring about being invited to parties. Can I live without all that? All the time and effort I've put into being popular is going to be wiped out in one swoop if I do this.

But I want it. So bad.

And as mad as I am at Edward, I understand why, because if it was him behaving this way, I'd think he was crazy. Caring about what people think over doing something you love. It sounds seriously messed up. Sam was right. I tell him how proud I am of him, being himself, but I can't even do it in my own life.

Well, that is going to change.

As of today, maybe, oh I don't know.

No, I am absolutely calling Mrs Gibson, and I am going to accept the interview. It will change my life, but I want to be happy, and I want people I love to be proud of me. No one is proud of me right now, least of all myself.

Speak of the devil, I watch him walk across the year 12 courtyard. How is it fair that he gets to look good in his own clothes and I'm stuck in this uniform? He looks so good, he runs into Coop, and they stop to chat. There is a sight to see right there. I see them catch the eye of a couple of the younger girls. The twin thing always gets them more attention, and looking like they do, I can't imagine anyone would walk past without giving them a second glance.

"Penny for them." I turn around and Heidi is standing there eyeing me her eyes narrowed.

"You don't want to know." I sigh

"With the look on your face, I don't need to. So, Edward or Cooper?"

"What are you talking about?"

"You're pining over one of them. My money is on Cooper." She whispers.

"What, why would you say that? I would never look at Cooper that way!" Never have I ever seen Cooper like that, which is weird, considering they're identical, but then, they have entirely different personalities.

"Ah-ha, I knew it, I totally knew it was Edward but had to get you to admit it."

I sigh, "Argh, guys shouldn't even be in my head right now. I have quite a day ahead of me."

"What, why? We'll get back to that in a minute, but the more important thing is you *are* thinking of guys right now, well...one guy. So what are you going to do about it? You know he likes you too."

"He doesn't. He can hardly bear to be anywhere near me."

"I'm going to lock you two in a room on your own, you'd soon sort it out. I mean, how many people have an actual den that they hang out, just the two of them. Give me your phone."

"No, I don't like the sound of that."

"Oh, you like being miserable?"

"Of course not, but there's stuff going on."

"Give me your phone now. No argument."

I've had enough. My head is going to explode. I hate it. Things between Edward and me are so awful. She's right, I need to sort it out.

I hand it over.

**Can we meet in the den tonight?** She texts Ed straight away.

I watch him read the message and scan the yard. His eyes land on me and we hold each other's gaze, he's trying to communicate something, but I have no idea what. It's as though there's no one else on the yard, only us.

He finally drags his eyes away from mine and goes to his phone.

**Of course, Buttercup**

I sag with relief. Tonight. We'll sort everything out tonight.

---

To everyone else, it seems like a regular school day, to me, it's monumental. I purposely don't seek out the popular crew at lunch but instead sit with Heidi, Anna and Rosie, Riley and their friends, and I actually relax and have fun. I'm myself. It feels good…liberating. They don't ask why I'm there. Rosie and Riley are aware that something is going on with me. I guess it will come out soon enough.

Heidi and Anna seem over the moon that I don't want to go to Chelsea. Maybe they've been suffering her because of me, that makes me sad. I didn't want to put pressure on them too. Well, at least that changes today.

---

Ed is on the bus on the way home. He doesn't say anything to me, but what he does is stroke down my arm, kind of a gentle pat, as we walk past. Again, trying to analyse, I'm not sure what it meant, other than maybe it was an olive branch.

As soon as I get home, I dial Mrs Gibson. She sounds ecstatic to hear from me.

"Oh love, I am so happy to hear from you. Are we all go on the interview? I realise it's short notice, but they want to do the interview tonight if you were going ahead. The reporter covering it is going on holiday tomorrow. I literally got off the phone with her five minutes ago."

My stomach lurches. Wow, this is going faster than I thought. Can I do this? Hell yes, I'm going to! I have had no time to prepare for the interview though, I'll have to wing it.

I agree and tell her I'll get the bus when I'm changed out of my uniform. She says no way she's sending her driver for me! Driver! This woman is seriously rich and soon I will have £50,000 in my bank account for Uni - and maybe a car and driving lessons, we will see, so I will be rich in my own way. Pete has said he'll take me for lessons when I get my provisional and pass my theory, but I still need official lessons and a car!

I get off the phone and hurry to get dressed. Hmmm, what to wear for an interview about gardening? This is a first. I chuckle to myself.

I message Ed. **Can we meet later? I have to do something?**

**Sure, everything OK?**

I bite my lip. I could use the moral support. I want Ed with me.

**I understand things are weird between us at the moment, but could you come with me somewhere? I could use the company.**

**Of course, Harp, where are we going?**

**Come over, I'll explain.**

I get dressed super quickly and touch up my make-up. I decide on blue leggings and a white fitted t-shirt, I don't want to look too dressy, but I don't want to seem like I haven't tried.

As I'm racing downstairs, there is a knock at the back door and front, simultaneously. I decide on the front door first. Ed can wait a minute. It's an older guy, dressed in normal clothes, but he hands me a pass. "Miss Lloyd, I'm here to take you to the Gibson residence. Here is my ID. I'm Simon." He smiles at me kindly, and I check his ID. It's a pass for security, but it has his picture on and a bar code.

"Hi, nice to meet you. Please come in, my friend is coming with me, and he's at the back door."

He nods and steps inside as I race to the back door, where I see Ed trying the handle, but the door is locked. I turn the key and open the door. "Hey." I breathe, trying to keep my calm.

He smiles when he sees me, "Hey, where were you?"

I step back so he will come in, "Follow me."

We walk through to the front door, grabbing my bag and phone on the way. "This is Simon. He's going to be taking us."

"What? Where are we going?"

I smile but say nothing and get him to follow me out so that I can lock the front door.

We climb into the car, both sitting in the back, side by side.

Edward turns to me, "Ok, you better tell me what this is about right now. Are you in the mafia?"

I turn in my seat so I'm facing him a little, "So I won the competition, and I know Sam told you that I was maybe going to turn it down, but I didn't. Mrs Gibson wants me to go around her place now to discuss the competition with the journalist from the local paper."

"Wow, this is all happening fast."

"Yeah, she's going on holiday or something. Anyway, guess I will be a local celebrity earlier than I thought."

He eyes at me with a look I can't fathom, then whispers, "I'm sorry." He shakes his head. "I should never have said those things to you. They were so uncalled for and for accusing you of doing that to Sam."

I glance at the driver, I don't want to get into this now. "We can talk later, yeah? But for now. Please hold my hand through this thing and don't let me say anything stupid."

He grabs hold of my hand - I didn't actually mean literally, but sparks fly and flow through my body at his touch - and we arrive at the most enormous iron gates ever. Ones I recognise from the pictures of this place. We're here.

*Deep breath, Harper.*

## Chapter Twenty-Four

Edward

I am so proud of her right now.

As we leave the Gibson residence, and oh my god, what a residence it is, we're both on a high. We ask the driver to take us to the village, and we have a milkshake while we talk about the interview.

Once we rehashed everything and decided that she hadn't said anything stupid, we went home.

We step outside. It's a sunny evening, still warm.

"So, what are you going to do with all your money?"

She grins that beautiful happy grin that I have missed so much. "Hmmm, I'm thinking motorbike, booze, partying - blow the lot."

"Well, that sounds like a great and sensible idea." She would never blow it in a million years.

"Ha. I'm probably going to put it away for Uni."

I nod, "You know what you're doing at Uni yet?"

She shakes her head, "no, but I'll need living costs whatever I do if I live away and Mum doesn't have any funding for it. Can't believe I'll be in sixth form in September. Exams start in a couple of weeks."

"Yeah, need to get right on that revising thing for my year one exams too. We could revise together?" I ask hopefully.

"I'd like that. Thank you for tonight, for being there for me."

"It may not seem like it these last few weeks, but I'll always be there for you, Harper."

She blinks, her big blue eyes conveying so much emotion. "Promise?"

I grab her hand and squeeze it. "I promise." We walk home together hand in hand, she doesn't remove her hand, and neither do I. To anyone looking in, we are teenagers in love.

"We still need to talk, right? Shall we go to the den?" she asks.

I have an idea.

"Yeah, but there's something I need to do first. Will you give me an hour and meet me in there at 9?"

She nods, "sure, no problem."

"In fact, don't go in there until I've texted you, k?"

"Ok, I'll do my homework, and mum might be home, so I can tell her about the competition."

We part ways and I run to my room and open my laptop. I stop for a moment. What to say…I start typing. Nervous that one way or another, mine and Harper's relationship is going to change.

*So, I heard you were mad at me. I'm sorry that I made you have those feelings. I never wanted you to feel as though you were being messed around. It couldn't have been further from the truth. This was my way of telling you my feelings without actually revealing my feelings. It was a coward's way out, but I couldn't cope any longer being in your life and you not knowing how I feel.*

*So... here it is. I love you, Harper. Guess I should tell you who I am right. This is the terrifying part because if you don't have feelings for me, things will be very awkward. But remember this, just like I told you five minutes ago, I'll always be there for you.*

*Yup, it's me, Buttercup.*

*Please don't be mad. I was so scared to tell you. I still am. It's something that happened gradually. A smile here, a laugh and a giggle there, the closeness we have that I will never have with anyone else. But the truth is, it's just you, everything about you. That is why I'm truly sorry for what I said because you are beautiful inside and out.*

*So this is me being brave (I'm very brave over email.) I guess that there is only one more thing I have left to say.*

*Meet me at our place.*

I sign off and schedule the send for 30 minutes, giving me enough time to go to the den and do what I want to do.

I go into my drawer. They're here somewhere. A couple of years ago, Harper did me an album of all pictures from when we were little to now and put them in an album for me. I find it and nip into mum's room. She won't mind if I borrow the fairy lights that she has around her dressing table. They'll be back before she realises they're missing.

I make my way outside.

It's still lightish, the sun is trying to set, and I spend the next twenty minutes hanging string and pegs and setting out the photographs so they hang all over the roof of the den. There's the one where we're sitting in our prams eating ice cream, covered in the stuff when we're around two. There's the one on the Queen's jubilee parade day float–we're both dressed as native Indians - there's one from Harper's first day of school with me and Cooper surrounding her as though we're going to protect her. There are birthday parties, fair rides, swimming pools, so many memories and hopefully, we will make more.

Final touches, I hang the fairy lights around the back wall and straighten the blankets and pillows. Wow, who knew I could be so romantic.

I check the time. My email went through two minutes ago. I stand outside and wait, hands in pockets, pretending that my entire world doesn't depend on my best friend's feelings and how she feels about me.

Any minute now she'll be here.

## Chapter Twenty-Five

♥

Harper

I finish reading the email and realise my mouth is open.

I re-read it. Edward loves me? My Edward? *Loves me*?

Ok, one more time, I re-read it. I don't believe this. He's in the den, waiting for me right now, and he's been *Rookiewithgirls* all along. I never even contemplated not for one second that it could have been him. I mean, we're best friends, why didn't he tell me.

I put my laptop down as I read those last words.

*"Meet me at our place."*

I need to go to him. Now.

I rush downstairs, "Mum, I'm going to the den."

I don't give her time to answer as I rush outside and down the garden. I go through the back gate, and my breath catches at my throat because there he is. My best friend, watching for my next move, waiting for my answer, wanting to know if we can be more.

I break into a run, and as I reach him, he goes back on one foot to steady us both.

His eyes are searching mine. "Well?"

I reach and brush a stray hair from his fringe out of his face. "Edward, why didn't you tell me?"

"I think we've established I'm a coward." He whispers.

"You're in love with me."

"I am." He whispers.

"Good, because I'm in love with you too."

The relief seems to overwhelm him, and he slowly closes his eyes and exhales. He opens them, a slow grin forming on his face. "You are?"

"Oh yeah. And that kiss? It was totally real for me."

He gives a slight nod as his hand comes up to cup my cheek. "Me too, Harper. Not been able to think of much else since."

My eyes drop to his mouth and back to his eyes. I run my tongue across my lips quickly, he sees it and his eyes flash. His thumb grazes my bottom lip as he glances at my mouth.

He leans his head in, so his mouth is nearly on mine. "Just to be clear, this one is real, right?"

"This one is real, Cap." And his mouth is on mine. Every nerve ending in my body comes to life as his soft lips land on mine. My Edward, my best friend, loves me, and I love him. And for God knows how long, I've fantasized this happening again and again, and now it's actually happening. He's mine. I reach my hands up and snake them around his neck, my fingers running through the hair there that is long and curling slightly. His hands on my waist slide around my back to draw me into him, pulling my body flush with his. Our mouths move and meld together, and the kiss deepens. We kiss and kiss. I could happily stay like this forever, suddenly euphoric as though I could conquer the world.

He makes a growling sound as I break apart from him. "Tell me again, Cap."

"I love you, Harper. I love you so much. I've wanted you for so long, to have you so close but not in this way. It's been torture."

"When did you realise that you liked me in this way?"

"Probably around a year ago. Do you remember when we were sunbathing, and we got the hosepipe out? I don't wanna sound shallow, but you in that black bikini, all wet from the hosepipe? I most definitely noted that you were more than friend material then, and it grew from there. Truth is, it's always been you. You've always been my person, my go-to. I have a twin brother, for crying out loud, but you're are still the one I choose to spend all my time with and talk to about anything. We fit." He pulls me back into his body and leans into my mouth, "in more ways than one." He kisses me firmly and then kisses down my chin and down my neck. Oh god, it's sublime, the best feeling *ever*. Ed is kissing my neck, and I never want it to stop. I fist my hand in his hair to hold his head there. His tongue darts out to lick my neck and nip at it with his teeth. "Hey."

He breaks off, smirking, "Sorry, you taste good enough to eat."

He grabs my hand and pulls me towards the den. "Come on, we still need to talk."

The scene before me takes my breath away. I can't believe he's done this. There are pictures of us all around, and the den is so pretty with all the fairy lights.

I turn to him, " You did all this?" I whisper.

He slides his arm around my waist, "Yeah, I want you to know how much you mean to me. All these memories and pictures are happy times with you, Harp, and imagine how many more we've got to make. I can't wait."

He smiles down at me with love in his eyes. I don't know how I haven't noticed it before. Guess we've both been blind.

"I thought about getting you flowers, but you hate it when flowers are picked."

He's so right, I do. We should leave them to grow–I hate it – it's murder.

"No, this is perfect."

He pulls out a glass for each of us, like a champagne glass, must be his parents, and a can of coke each.

He pours our glasses and motions for me to sit down, and he does the same.

He grabs his glass and chinks it with mine. "To us, whatever the future may hold for us, we'll always have each other."

"To us," I say, my eyes smiling.

We have our drink, we may have another kiss. Not telling. Then we talk. Obviously, he knows now that I overheard him all those years ago, and he explains he was a child, and it meant nothing.

As we're lying there, staring at the photographs on the roof and fairy lights, contentment washes over me. I'm right where I'm supposed to be.

"This has always been my safe place. I can't believe I'm here with my boyfriend now."

"Yeah, we're gonna have some explaining to do to our parents. They're gonna worry we've been getting up to stuff in here."

"My mum won't care. Yours may have something to say, we know the truth. I hope they don't stop us coming in here, though."

He shakes his head and holds his arm out, motioning me to go over to him. I shimmy over, and his arm closes around me. I rest my head on his shoulder.

"This is nice."

"It's perfect."

"Our place."

## Final Chapter

♥

Harper

I glance at Edward as I sit next to him on the bus. "Things are going to change for me at school after all this Chelsea stuff. You sure you want to be seen with the geeky girl and not some cool girl?"

He nods and leans down to kiss me, "Oh, I'm sure."

Cooper and some of the others groan. "Seriously, is this how it's going to be now?"

Liam speaks, "Yeah, every time I turn around, you're sucking each other's faces off."

"Hey, we have a lot of catching up to do." I narrow my eyes at Cooper.

He rolls his eyes, "You two are the worst, you have taken forever to get here."

"At least we're here now, Coop," Ed says and grins at me with a soft smile.

Rosie and Riley were so happy for me when I texted them. I've promised to give them all the details later.

We're sitting in assembly when I hear my name. What? I was drifting off, my mind on other things. What was it he was saying?

"So this talented junior member of our school community has done amazing things. She is an inspiration to others."

He isn't talking about me, is he?

I shoot a look at Sam, who I'm sitting next to, his eyes wide.

"The competition that Harper has won, over adults all over the country, Is a credit to her. Harper, do you want to come up and stand in front of the school?"

Oh god, no.

I slowly stand and walk to the front. The headteacher turns to me. "Well done, Harper, truly an impressive achievement."

I'm sure you will be seeing Harper in more newspapers and headlines over the coming years. Her gardening abilities and knowledge certainly astounds me.

Everyone claps, and I hurriedly sit back in my spot, but not before seeing Edward sitting with the sixth formers, clapping and grinning at me. Before I sit down, he winks at me.

If he did this, I'll kill him.

He didn't do it, it turned out. The newspaper called to school for a quote on how I am academically, so they got wind of the competition that way.

I look around for Ed after grabbing my lunch from the cafeteria. We can't seem to separate after everything. We talked so much last night, and I ended up sneaking back into the house at 11.30. So tired today, but it was so worth it.

I am in love world! With the hottest guy in school! And he loves me!

I spot him on a table and go over. I lean into his hear, "Hey gorgeous."

His head turns, and when he sees it's me, he spins his whole body around, parting his legs, so I'll step in them.

"Hey beautiful, how's your day?"

I look up, "Pretty much perfect. Yours?"

"Same! How weird." He smiles at me, "Come here, I want a kiss."

"Say please."

"Come on, you know you need the practice."

I frown and bat him on the shoulder.

I do as he asks, though and lean down to kiss him, just as Chelsea walks over. Great.

"So, it's true, about you two?"

I turn to her, "Hey Chelsea." I sound bored.

I'm still finding my footing on this being who I want to be business, but I absolutely love the part where I don't have to suck up to her anymore. I can sound bored now - because she does bore the hell out of me.

Edward stands but turns me so we're both facing her, and he has his hands around my waist. "Yeah, Chelsea, it's true, we decided to take the friend thing up a notch."

"Well, nice of you to tell me."

"It was never anything with us, Chelsea, I made that clear," Edward says, a lot calmer than I am.

She narrows her eyes at him and then fixes her gaze on me, "So gardening, huh? You kept that quiet?"

I shrug, "I've been caring a little too much about what people think. I've decided to turn over a new leaf and do what makes me happy instead?"

Her lips curl in disgust, "So having your hand in soil with bugs and stuff makes you happy."

I nod, "Actually, yeah, it does."

"Each to their own, but all this geek you've been hiding probably means you'll lose all of your friends. They're not gonna wanna hang with the weird gardening chick."

Edward stiffens behind me. He's done talking to Chelsea, but I can defend myself.

"Actually, my real friends - the ones who really know me - will love that I've done this, instead of acting like a superficial, stuck-up bitch, I can now actually be myself."

She gasps.

Done with this conversation, I turn to Ed, whose eyes are twinkling, a small smile playing on his lips.

"Shall we move tables, Cap?"

He nods, "Wherever you will go, I will follow. Lead the way."

So, I do.

# *Epilogue*

♥

Cooper

I shake my head and smile at the floor, proud of Harper that she stood up to Chelsea. I thought trouble might go down today with her and wanted to hang around to check she was ok, see if they needed any backup. They seem fine. They don't need me after all.

I leave the two love birds to their lunch and walk towards the music room. My favourite place to be. I am way too early for the room to be open yet for lesson, but I can sit outside and wait for the teacher to open up.

I usually skip lunch altogether. If I get the teacher before lunch, he lets me stay in there to work on my music.

I hear some notes coming from the music room. To one end, there is actually a full-on recording booth. The music is coming from there.

I stop and listen. *Sweet child o' mine* is being played on the electric guitar and sounds impressive. Wow. Who is this? And why don't I know about it? I'm aware of everyone at this school that can play.

I'm about to step inside and check who it is when Harper's friend, Anna, shouts me. I turn around and raise my eyebrows at her. Never spoken to this girl in my life. What does she want?

She catches up to me. "Cooper, hey! Please can you come with me? Edward needs you."

She is out of breath, and her eyes are darting everywhere except for at me.

I frown. He was fine a minute ago. "Are you sure?"

She shrugs. "Sure, he wanted you for something. He said as soon as possible."

I grunt. "Fine."

I wanted to find out who was playing the guitar like that. I reluctantly follow Anna. This better be important.

I finally find Edward, who is standing with Harper behind the science block. They don't seem upset. In fact, they look on cloud nine. About bloody time too, these two have been messing around for way too long. Thank god they've finally admitted their feelings for each other. I couldn't stand it for much longer.

"Ed," I shout to get his attention.

Ed looks up from Harper and frowns at me. "What's up, bro?"

"*You* wanted *me*."

He shakes his head. "No, I didn't. What are you talking about?"

I point to Harper, "Her friend, Anna, is it? She said you needed me urgently?"

He shakes his head, frowning. "Maybe she got mixed up."

Harper's eyes widen as she glances over my shoulder. I turn around and see Anna with Harper's other friend Heidi. Her eyes meet mine through those dark-rimmed glasses of hers, and she immediately looks down to the floor.

Edward shouts to Anna. "Why did you tell Coop that I wanted him?"

Her eyes flit between everyone as she bites her lip. What is going on?

She speaks, "Er…um."

Harper speaks, "Oh, I know - earlier I asked her that if she saw you, could she get you to come find us. Sorry, it doesn't matter now, nothing important."

This all reeks of a lie. I assess Harper's friends. Heidi still staring at the floor, her bobbed hair falling to cover her face, and her other friend seems like she's going to faint on the spot under my stare.

I shake my head. "Whatever. Later."

So annoyed that I now don't have a clue who was playing in the studio.

I turn around and head back to music. There's a chance they might still be there.

<u>Heidi</u>

My shoulders drop as he walks off. Thank god. That was a close one. He almost caught me. I thought he wasn't going to music today, that I'd be safe to have a practice, and Mr Ball said it would be ok. It's too risky playing at school now. I'd die if anyone knew. My music is for me and no one else, no matter how much Mr Ball keeps trying to get me to play in front of people.

If Cooper heard me, it would be game over. He unnerves me with that talent of his. He doesn't know that I've listened to him on the drums, no one does, but I have…so many times. He can never find out how I feel about him…

## Also By MJ Ray

♥

Meet Me at the Bus Stop (Rosie and Liam's Story) Book 1

Meet Me at the Gym (Riley and Russ' Story) Book 2

*If you want to keep up to date on any coming releases, beta reader offers, or other things, then please sign up to my newsletter here.*

*Thank you so much for reading my novel. I hope you enjoyed it! The best way to thank an author for writing a great book is to leave an honest review. I would be so grateful if you did that.*

If
you want to connect with me:

Facebook: https://www.facebook.com/MJ-Ray-Author-106849384519134

Amazon Author Page: https://www.amazon.com/MJ-Ray/e/B08LDWNL9W/ref=dp_byline_cont_pop_ebooks_1

E-mail: authormjray@outlook.com

Bookbub: MJ Ray Books - BookBub